I0659471

DRAGONS OF WELLSDEEP

DAWN BLAIR

MORNING SKY STUDIOS

Copyright © 2021, 2024 by Dawn Blair

All rights reserved.

ISBN: 978-0-9985441-7-5

No part of this book may be reproduced in any form or by any electronic or mechanical means, including information storage and retrieval systems, without written permission from the author, except for the use of brief quotations in a book review.

The story and characters are entirely fictional. Any resemblance to actual events, persons (living or dead), or locales is purely coincidental.

Cover and layout copyright © 2021 by Morning Sky Studios
Cover design by Dawn Blair/Morning Sky Studios
Cover art copyright © Ingus Kruklitis | Dreamstime.com, © Digitalstormcinema | Dreamstime.com, and © Kalcutta | Dreamstime.com

Morning Sky Studios
PO Box 5422
Twin Falls, ID 83303
Visit us at www.morningskystudios.com

ALSO BY DAWN BLAIR:

Stonecharmer

Stonecharmer

Stonebreaker

Stonesinger

Onesong

Palladium

Tangled Magic

Walk the Path

Sacred Knight

Quest for the Three Books

Manifest the Magic

To Birth a Destiny

History of a Dead Man (companion novella)

Prince of the Ruined Land

The Missing Thread

Sword and Shield

The Unicorn and the Secret (companion novella)

The Loki Adventures

1-800-Mischief

For Sale, Call Loki

For A Good Time, Call Loki

For More Information, Call Loki

For More Mischief, Call Loki

1-800-CallLoki (Omnibus of novellas 1-5)

1-800-IceBaby

Help Wanted, Call Loki

1-800-Lok8

Dressed to the 9's

Wells of the Onesong stories

Fractured Echo

Fall's Confession

The Doorway Prince

Stardust

Mystery of the Stardust Monk

Alexander's Den

PROLOGUE

Her time of merely watching drew to a close. Soon, she'd take the child.

The little boy headed to the well. Submerged, she watched him in the reflection of the water's surface, a waving mirage with the blue sky behind him. He stomped his feet as he walked, pounding on the ground like a heartbeat. She felt his restrained temper tantrum mixing with her own pulse in a growing, synchronized cacophony with his irritation.

"Get a bucket of water for me," his mother had asked. He'd had to leave his toys, leaving the wooden pieces lifelessly scattered around where he'd been playing in order to go fulfill his chore.

The boy drew closer to the well. The lurker waited for the shadow of his cherub face to look down into the water. Why did he delay? She reached out, touching upon his young and undefined emotions.

"Yesssss," she hissed, her forked tongue giving a flicker against her sharp teeth. "Make a wissshhhhh."

The boy tapped the outer edge of the well with his toes

as he arrived. Dirt clouded in the air. "I wish…" the boy began. He set his bucket down on the ground and pulled the well's bucket from the hook on the post.

"Yessss!" She watched the boy lean over the surface.

"I wish I didn't have to get water anymore." He took the well bucket and dropped it down into the well.

"Oh, my beautiful boy, I can make your wish come true," she whispered from beneath the water. "Just show me that you can feel the connection between us and you will never have to draw water from the well again."

His cheeks puffed with air as he hauled the bucket from free the well, an act which took all his might to turn the crank. He reached over to grab the bucket loaded with water. His long, wavy, black hair dangled around the sides of his face as he glanced down and she looked up at him. Oh, the sweetness of him, this little child.

The boy paused, as if noticing something under the surface of the water.

She smiled. "Yessss. Lean closer."

Did he yet know that he belonged to her?

No, but he soon would.

The boy set the bucket on the short wall of the well, then leaned over the edge, trying to see what he'd glimpsed before. His young, round face looked momentarily confused as he realized that the level of the water was much higher than he'd ever seen before. He couldn't explain it the water displacement, but she knew.

She knew the well was his destiny.

As the confusion eased from his face into delightful wonder, his blue eyes took on a moon crest shape as his pudgy cheeks lifted with a smile. The tight spiral curls swung as if they were a fairy's delight.

"You sense me. We are connected." She stared back at

him. "You are beautiful," she said to him through the water as her own babies swam toward him eagerly.

The boy gazed back, his fingers reaching toward the little swirls he saw in the water. He could see them, her young hatchlings. He drew back with a moment of panic and looked inside his bucket. Satisfied that none of the swirls had gone into his water, he returned to the well and dangled his fingers into the water. The hatchlings nibbled at his fingers and the boy laughed.

"Beautiful," he said, poking his finger in the water at one of the hatchlings.

The beast waiting beneath the surface fully opened her dragon eyes. The light of this world was harsh, a golden yellow, and the same color as her eyes without the glare shielding. Of course, she had returned to this spot as the very place she had been spawned. Now it was her turn to find a protector for her children as her mother had once done.

The boy gasped when he saw her looking up at him. He lost his handhold on the stone and fell backwards off the wall.

She rose from the water, her children splashing back down into the well as she flew out. The boy brushed his curly black hair away from his tanned face with chubby fingers. He was so beautiful.

"Thank you," she whispered to Father Sun and Mother Moon.

The boy stood frozen in fear.

She ate him head first in one bite. Just perfect.

Then she spread her wings, watching as the yellow sun flashed off her red scales, and took flight into the late afternoon sky. Her hatchlings were left behind, and she had what she'd come for.

TEN YEARS LATER...

The cave shook with the dragon's moan as another convulsion swept over her. The contractions were becoming stronger now.

"The stomach vent is opening," a sapere yelled as she carefully lifted one of the dragon scales. "It's big. This one is going to be strong."

"Vehlka, you're doing great," another sapere added as he soaked a cloth and squeezed it out over the dragon's head. But he threw a furtive glance at the other sapere not far away.

The sapere shook her head.

"Ahhhh!" the dragon screamed.

The stomach vent opened and the sapere got splashed in a wet gooey mass. She quickly got up and rinsed herself in another bucket nearby and went back to her position. Blood lay all around the dragon, dribbling from the stomach vent and growing in a thick pool on the floor.

"Come on, Vehlka," the sapere shouted to be heard over the dragon's agony. "It's free of the lining. You just have to push now."

The dragon heard the faint rumble of engines as a small craft landed outside the caves. He had made it in time.

Vehlka's red tail thrashed as another contraction gripped her. The male sapere got knocked backwards.

"Push, Vehlka!" the sapere still at the dragon's side screamed.

The dragon rolled onto her belly and reared her head back.

"He'sss not coming!" the dragon raged. "Balthier!"

A man appeared in the arched entryway to the cave. "I'm here, Vehlka."

"Do it!"

The man, Balthier, put his hand to the hilt of his dagger as he came forward.

The sapere jumped to her feet and ran to block him from further entering the cave. "You can't. She's a Ch'bauldi and you are charged to protect her."

"She's more than that," Balthier growled. "She's my novimather. Now get out of my way."

The sapere hurried to stand behind the female sapere. Balthier looked them over, realizing neither of the saperes were going to stand down. He grimaced and gave a little shake of his head. "Thirty seconds," he muttered, having assessed his opponents.

The male sapere drew back in fear, moving toward the dragon as he obviously had the sense to fear a novihomidrak, but the other sapere reached for Balthier's dagger.

Balthier shrugged, blocking the sapere's attempt at seizing his weapon. "Very well, twenty seconds and I'll use Harmony." He backhanded the sapere with his right hand while his left grabbed his dagger from the sheath. Along the blade in the language of the ancient dragons was the word *Harmony*.

As the woman dropped to the cave floor, the male sapere made one last feeble effort to stop the novihomidrak, who just knocked him aside.

Balthier flowed toward the dragon and, before his knees had hit the ground, he sank Harmony into the dragon's flesh right below the stomach vent. He jerked aside the scale below the blade and continued the tear. Ooze slithered out. He took another scale off. Blood spurted like water rushing over a dam.

Then, a long oval pearl slid out across the slimy, blood-covered cave floor.

The dragon moaned with pain and relief as she turned to look at the egg. "He isss beautiful still."

The pearl shimmered. The dragon raised her forearm and looked to be about to smash it.

Balthier put his hand on the one black claw she held extended toward the shell. "Vehlka, don't. He must do this if he is to have his strength. Do not rush it because of your fate."

"Just a touch to aid him," she begged. But when Balthier shook his head, she set to watching the pearl as it began to rock back and forth on the floor. The blood from the hard birthing vanished from the shell as if someone had come along and wiped it clean.

Vehlka set her head down on the floor. Balthier reached out and put his hand on her neck. He noticed the saperes trying to stop the bleeding from the incision caused by *Harmony*.

"He is my pevitias," Vehlka said, "my final blessed novihomidrak. He shall take with him my magic."

"Do you have the strength to heal yourself?" Balthier asked, wishing he didn't already know the answer.

"Not if I am to name him and his weaponsss."

"Put your magic in that then. Bless him and make this novi your pevitias." Balthier picked up the cloth the sapere had been using on the dragon and wiped the dragon's head.

One of the saperes began to huff with indignation, but Balthier turned a hard glare at them before the protesting whine started. The hush gave way to the sound of Vehlka's labored breathing and the pearl rocking on the cave floor.

The shell around the pearl cracked.

"He will sparkle, won't he?" Vehlka said.

Balthier hesitated before nodding his head. "He does." He pushed away the thought that he'd been called here for Vehlka's pevitias. Anyone but him. Certainly Vehlka knew he'd make a terrible mentor for a novihomidrak, let alone her pevitias.

A heavy thump came from inside the pearl, making it threaten to roll all the way over rather than just wobble. But before it could move, the shell started to crumble, revealing a boy now fifteen with long curly black hair. As the shell collapsed, it attached itself to the skin of the boy who lay curled on the floor.

"You will train him, yesss?" Vehlka asked.

Balthier thought he might be ill. Did the Ch'bauldi dragon know what she was asking of him? "I will. Don't worry about that." He swallowed the bile choking his words.

"Don't let him know he is my pevitias. You must treat him like an ordinary novihomidrak. Let him discover his destiny on his own."

Balthier nodded, still too sick to speak. What did he know about training another novihomidrak? This task Vehlka asked of him was too large and he was certainly not worthy.

"Do you think he knowsss my worry?"

"Not now, but he will know your other worries."

The dragon got quiet. For a moment, Balthier wondered if Vehlka was already dead. How would this child fair if she did not name him? Would the saperes' magic be enough? He doubted it. Then she opened her eyes and slid back the glare shield. She looked to the dome of open sky above where the moon rose overhead.

"I call him Moonhunter and his protections will be Serenity and Tranquility."

The words flowed as gold writing from her lips and floated through the air to the teen lying on the floor. The shrunk as they lowered down onto his chest. As they sank in, sparkling black lines grew across his arms and face. They lasted but a moment before disappearing.

The dragon sighed and placed her head on the floor. "Watch over your dragon brother."

"I will, and I will miss you too, Vehlka," Balthier said. "Thank you, my dragon mother."

The teen coughed as air entered his lungs. Vehlka moved, the desire to see her novihomidrak giving her renewed energy. Balthier went to aid Moonhunter to a sitting position.

The saperes began to wail.

The teen opened his dark brown eyes which shined with bright gold flecks which matched Vehlka's eyes. The dragon smiled at seeing this, then closed her eyes and lay down to rest for the final time.

1

Horrible, high-pitched shrieks pressed in around him. Moonhunter closed his eyes against the cruel light and slapped his hands over his ears from the harsh sound. The floor beneath him felt cold and wet. His whole body shivered. No, he trembled much more violently than merely being cold. He'd been through something traumatic. His body now responded to disposing itself of the excess energy. How did he know that so clearly when he didn't know what else was going on around him?

Hands grabbed him and raised his shoulders from the floor.

Eyes still tightly shut, Moonhunter's hands curled into claws and he blindly scratched at the person attacking him.

"You need to move," came a voice from the person behind him who Moonhunter was trying to strike.

Moonhunter looked back to see a wizened face covered with a graying brown beard and brown eyes hardened by trials of more than his age.

"Get up," shouted the gruff older man.

Moonhunter scrambled to his feet. The man dropped a

fur-lined coat over him. Only then did Moonhunter realize he'd been naked. As he clenched the coat close to him, he nearly slipped in the goo- covered floor. He twisted, seeing the large dragon's head near him and he nearly spilled over again.

"Easy there," the man said, catching him.

"W-what's going on?" Moonhunter asked.

"Ah, good. You can speak. Sometimes the dragons get overly ambitious and take someone too young to even speak yet."

Two people stretched themselves over the dragon's body and wailed again.

Moonhunter took a careful step, trying to get his bare feet out of the blood and ooze covering the floor. "What are they doing?"

"Do you know what they are?"

At first, Moonhunter wasn't certain why this man was asking him a question rather than giving the answer he'd requested, but he felt an energy move through him which seemed to remove the curtain from his own knowing. "They're saperes, wise ones, blessed by dragon magic."

"Good. You recognize their true nature. More will come." The man turned Moonhunter away from the sight. "Welcome, Moonhunter. You are now one of the most noble and respected creatures in the universe: a novi-homidrak."

"A what?"

He seemed a little disappointed that he had to explain. "Novihomidrak. A human born from a dragon. It's what you are, what I am. You can put those away now. No one here will hurt you."

Moonhunter looked down in the direction the man pointed and saw short, black nail buds growing out of his fingers. How was he supposed to put them away?

The man held up his hand, giving Moonhunter a wry smile visible through straight cuts made for his mouth in his coarse brown beard. Moonhunter gaped as lengthy, round, claws appeared from the tips of the man's fingers. "I'll be impressed when yours get as long as mine."

The man led him over to an altar where several items sat. He picked up a stone. "Here, hold this."

Moonhunter was still trying to figure out how to get his claws to retract when the stone landed in his palm. It instantly went orange and nearly dropped Moonhunter to the ground. The man caught his hand and took the stone from it.

"Very good. Your novimather would be proud."

"My novimather?"

"Dragon mother." The man pointed to the dragon still being cried over by the saperes. Moonhunter tried to think. He'd been having one of the strangest dreams for such a long time. But he felt like he'd woken to a stranger world.

The man picked up a dagger, which looked ornamental in nature, but still had a sharp blade. Moonhunter was just beginning to feel the threat when the man threw the dagger at him. It went through his coat. Moonhunter felt the dagger, but it didn't cut him. The blade bounced off him and fell to the floor.

"There is barely any weapon made that can hurt you now." The man picked up Moonhunter's hand and pushed back the sleeve of the coat to reveal his arm, which glowed as a gold and white netting moved over the flesh. "You've been given a dragon shell. Only weapons forged by dragons, saperes of other dragon clans, or other novihomidraks can pierce your skin."

"I don't..."

"Understand, I know. Okay, here we go. History 101. Everything I wish I'd been told when I waked from the dragon-birthing. Keep your own notes, kid. When your mother's hatchlings call you back for a birth of their own, you'll want to remember what to tell the new novi-homidrak."

The man turned him around to face the dead dragon once more. "You were born a human in your Life-Before. Judging from your age, I'd say you were around four to five cycles of your planet's orbit. You had a human mother. She has mourned your loss a long time ago and would not recognize you if she saw you. There is no sense in looking for her."

"I don't remember any of that."

"Good. You'll understand why in a moment. Vehlka had just laid her dragon eggs. "

"Vehlka?"

"Your novimather."

Moonhunter looked at the dragon, sadness gripping him. "Do they always die?"

"No," the man said, turning him around again. They began to walk down a tunnel leading from the cave. "Vehlka was old. You are her seventh dragon-birthed. She knew you would be her last. That's why she called me to be here. But I get ahead of myself."

The tunnel shifted to a hallway. Moonhunter tried to look at the transition from stone to wood, and even glanced back the way they had come, but the man pulled him along.

The man continued, "With her eggs laid, Vehlka had a limited time in order to choose. Somehow, she happened upon you and choose you. She swallowed you whole, where you would slide into a special nesting place inside her. Sometimes the seedlings don't take. You obviously did. For about ten of our years, since Ch'bauldi dragons mark time with their home sun, you have been gaining all the knowledge and wisdom of the Ch'bauldi dragons. You are more than a vessel for their knowledge though; you are a child of the Ch'bauldi. You don't know it yet, but you now understand the secrets of the Wells."

"The Wells?"

"Focus on that word for a moment. The answer will come to you."

Moonhunter assessed the man warily, then closed his eyes. "The Wells," he whispered to get himself to focus. At first, there was only darkness, then he started to see bright flashes of light. He didn't even have the words to describe the colorful nebulas and thousands of stars rippling across the universe. Black space of nothingness seemed to hold it all together like a spider's web. Moonhunter opened his eyes. "The Wells are the connections between worlds. It's like a pipeline."

"Very good," said the gruff man. He extended his arm out and put it around Moonhunter's shoulders to guide him along. "My name is Balthier. Your training starts now."

2

Moonhunter's arms dangled loosely in front of him as he ran forward while keeping himself as low to the ground as he could. Fifty meters to the speedster and only sparse, rocky cover between him and the machine.

Once he was there…

No, he had to stay focused on getting to the craft. Stay present. Balthier had scolded him often for getting ahead of himself. A flaw in his character, Balthier would tell him, or rather would shout at him while slapping him in the back of the head. Be mindful!

So, instead of planning what he'd do when he got to the speedster, he was reminiscing over past lectures. How exactly was someone supposed to be present in every moment?

A shot blasted apart a rock at his foot. As grit scattered all over his leather moccasin, Moonhunter reacted by raising his own PR387 blaster. In the middle of his reflexive action, another shot whizzed behind him. His forward jump sent his own shot wild and off-target. There were two snipers out there, but not professionals.

Moonhunter slid on the gravel, slipping and falling behind the shielding metal of the speedster. Rocks scraped against his flesh, trying to tear his skin, but the dragon shielding protected him. Still, the natural armament didn't stop the abrasion from hurting.

He reached up for the handle on the speedster's door and found it locked. "Damn," he muttered as he pulled Tranquility out of her sheath. He flipped to sit back on his heels, trying to keep his head down behind the speedster's window.

Balthier ran up to him and crouched beside him. "Did you get it?" Balthier's gruff voice asked.

"Would I be here if I hadn't?" Moonhunter shoved the dagger's blade between the metal of the cockpit window and the body of the speedster.

"Come on. What's taking so long?"

"Your informant locked it," Moonhunter growled.

"What? No?" Balthier gave a tug on the handle. "Son of a bitch!"

A blast shattered the cockpit window. Balthier reached through just as Moonhunter bore his weight on the dagger and started to inch the locking mechanism over. As Balthier pulled the release from inside, the cockpit's top popped open. Moonhunter lifted it. Another shot took out the window on the other side. Heedless of the glass, Moonhunter jumped into the back seat while Balthier took the front. Moonhunter reached up and pulled the frame of the cockpit lid down while Balthier fired the speedster up. The engine turned, but didn't fire.

"Just needs more ether," Balthier shouted as he repeatedly pushed a button on a console near his knees.

"I think your informant set us up. " Moonhunter slid down in his seat to keep his head out of view while he popped the used cartridge of his PR387 and slid a fresh one in. Then he turned to look out where the shots were being fired at them.

"He did not. His information has been good before."

"He wanted your god-damned hand stuck in the cookie jar this time, Balthier." Moonhunter shouted as another bullet pinged off the metal. "They're coming over the rise."

"Watch your language." Balthier tugged on the choke again and pushed the firing button. The engine sputtered.

"Now you've flooded it!" Moonhunter fired shots, blue beams trailing from his gun and hitting his targets. Once the three men coming over the ridge realized they were being fired upon, they scattered behind rocks. "My shot hit. They've got a novihomidrak with them."

"They're probably all novihomidraks!" Balthier had raised up on the seat so he could bear his full weight down on the pedals he was trying to push down. "Clutch is stuck. That's why it won't start."

"Maybe we need to make a run for it before this bucket of bolts becomes our casket."

"Just about got –" A blast rocked the ship as a shot exploded against the bottom. Knocked sideways, Balthier's head knocked into the metal cockpit frame.

"Balthier!" Moonhunter reached over the seat for Balthier as the gruff man slunk down in his harness, unconscious.

"Damn you, old man." Moonhunter slammed back into his seat and hit his own clutch petal. He pulled the choke with one hand while setting the throttle with the other. Hopefully Balthier hadn't flooded the engine too badly. He pushed the fire button and the engine came to life. "Leave it to someone who actually likes flying!"

Glass rolled over the floor around his feet as Moonhunter pushed forward on the elevation lever with his right hand and the ship began to rise with a slight yaw to the left. He jerked the steering wheel with this left hand and the wheel popped off the column.

Wind blew into Moonhunter's wide eyes as he stared at the bolt hitting the floor and the steering wheel in his lap.

Holding the steering wheel, Moonhunter blinked, lowering his dragon's lids over his eyes. His sight filled with the sharp clarity of dragon vision.

The speedster had turned just enough now that they were heading back the way they had come. Moonhunter could see his attackers now. Three men on the ridge with cloaks of tanned hide, though one had a cloak of white and black fur. He seemed to be yelling at the other two men, who hoisted onto their shoulders a large blaster while a shaky mechanical arm loaded another round into it.

Moonhunter tossed the steering wheel. He watched the round metal crash into the loading arm, dropping little chunks of metal into the blaster. As the mechanisms went to slide the ammunition door shut, the bits of the steering wheel stuck in the hatch, not allowing it to close.

The speedster tightened in on its circle. They were going to roll. He wasn't sure Balthier was buckled in. If he let go of the elevation lever, they would plummet back to the ground, bounce, and probably roll. Moonhunter stood and reached over Balthier's seat.

Fighting with his shoulders in the small space, he grasped for the front steering wheel. His first reach missed. He got it on the second. The ship stopped its roll, but was headed back toward the ground. He bent his knee and felt for the base of the lever with his foot. Finding it, he used his knee to nudge it forward. Except it wasn't a nudge.

The ship shot upward.

The two men dropped the weapon, scrambling away from it, while the third reached for the arch of the steering wheel jammed into it. Just before the ship had ascended too far, Moonhunter saw the fur-cloaked man kick the weapon before the view slid out of sight. A moment later, he heard the explosion behind him.

Balthier groaned and reached up to his head. "What happened?" he asked with slow, slurred speech.

"Saving your butt again, old man."

Balthier shifted and looked up at him. "Is that how you drive now, you mindless twit? Give me that." He sat up and took ahold of the wheel.

Moonhunter sat back down in his seat. "That's gratitude for you."

"Did you get a look at them?" Balthier asked after they were clear of their attackers.

Moonhunter knew he meant the people who'd been attacking them. "They were cloaked in hides. One definitely had to be a novihomidrak because he wasn't afraid of their rocket blaster backfiring on him. But he wasn't using his weapons against us either. Guess he may have only had hand-held weapons."

"Local mercenaries, it sounds like." Balthier said as he landed the rickety craft next to where his spacecraft sat.

"Probably. You think our informant hired them?" Moonhunter unlocked his seat belt and jumped out behind Balthier.

"I doubt it. Someone else was probably expecting us, someone who knew enough to hire a novihomidrak for his own side."

Moonhunter stopped in his tracks, several paces

behind, disbelieving as Balthier opened up his craft. "Come on, Balthier. That ship was in pretty bad condition, all but disabled. They knew if it crashed, we'd walk away. I think the informant wanted to have his cake and eat it too." He glanced back at the speedster.

Balthier laughed as he climbed inside. "Old world clichés! Aren't you just getting to be the regular book beast?" Balthier reached up and grabbed one of the black grab handles dangling from the ceiling though he didn't need to. The action was probably more from habit, as was his fingers moving over the keypad by the door.

Moonhunter hated it when his Balthier mocked him. Balthier couldn't understand his reasons, so why even bother?

"You going to take the prize back to the informant?" Moonhunter asked, closing the door behind him as he got into the bay.

Balthier pulled the blue and white sea stone from his pocket. It wasn't quite perfectly round, but more of an oval which had been shaped by compression, then polished by gentle washing in the planet's ocean for a few thousand years. "Still not sure why anyone would want a rock so badly."

"Maybe that's a question we should be asking?" Moonhunter added, hoping to guide Balthier back to the right course of action, which was to keep the sea stone until they knew more. "Maybe it was at the museum for more than just display too. It was well kept."

"You think?"

Moonhunter wasn't sure if Balthier was being sarcastic or serious, but before the returning quip left his mouth, a voice came over the telecom.

"Sir," the computer's feminine voice said smoothly,

"the ship is prepared. Launch protocols require your presence now."

"On my way, Rhonda," Balthier responded, already walking for the door to the forward cabin.

"Rhonda? You've given the ship a name?" Moonhunter asked.

Balthier gave a frisky grin. "We spend so much time in her, I thought it might be good to give her a name. Besides, it could throw someone off our trail if we said, 'Get back to Rhonda,' instead of, 'Get back to the ship.'"

"Whatever, old man. You can call her Rhonda. I'll be in back if you need me," Moonhunter said, heading in the opposite direction. He slipped inside his quarters and shut the door, knowing that he had until they landed to prepare.

T ake off consisted of little more than watching out
the windows for other ships while the computer
did most of the work. Balthier set the holograph
display of what was going on outside his craft in addition
to the visual screens he had set.

"Add all sublayer functions," Balthier said as the image
took form on the round projector plate. He watched the
image ripple as infrared, radar, and several other sensing
frequencies layered over the top of the hologram.

"Are you ready?" the computer asked.

No, he wasn't. He should have ordered Moonhunter to
get them into the air. Balthier was good at flying, but that
certainly didn't mean he liked it. Proficiency didn't give
way to passion. Not that he wanted to be limited to Well
travel either though. Space travel was a necessary evil.

So why hadn't he asked Moonhunter to administer
their takeoff?

Balthier glanced back even though he'd already heard
the door to Moonhunter's room shut. After every mission,
the boy had been disappearing into his quarters and he'd

rarely come out until after the flight. Was he experiencing flight sickness? Balthier didn't see how that could be possible, not when the boy loved flying so much, much more than himself. So what could Moon be doing?

"Are you ready?" the computer queried again.

"Rhonda, do you track any ships near us?" Balthier asked.

"None, sir."

"What's Moonhunter doing in his quarters?"

"Unknown," Rhonda replied. "He has not logged onto any shipboard systems."

Balthier sat for another moment. No games, no entertainment streaming, no communications, no books, no food. Was it possible Moon was just getting some sleep?

"Are you ready?"

"Yes," Balthier snapped at the interruption pulling him from his thoughts again. "Damn computer. Yes, Rhonda, let's go."

He watched the hologram. No ships. But he couldn't stop the nagging feeling inside him.

Balthier pulled the blue and white stone from his pocket and examined it. Through his dragon lids, the stone only seemed to sparkle a little bit more, but that was from the quartz so firmly pressed into it, nothing magical. There truly didn't seem to be anything significant about this stone other than it had been protected in one of the planet's museums.

The ship accelerated as it broke orbit.

There was still nothing on the holographic projection which indicated that they were being followed. Why was there no pursuit?

Balthier closed his fist around the stone, gripping it tightly. Not even a sense of magic. He released all of his emotions and let his energy just flow out as though going along the Humline to seek for the answers that he wanted. The mercenaries had been lying in wait for them, he knew it and the Humline confirmed it. But why? Why had they not been more organized? Why did they not continue the chase?

Why had a novihomidrak, even a mercenary who knew where to expect them, not be prepared for novihomidraks and bring the appropriate weapons to down them? Unless, someone wanted them alive and didn't want any mess ups. But what purpose would that serve? Imprisoning a novihomidrak was always dangerous business.

The computer beeped. "Incoming message," Rhonda followed.

Balthier tapped his fingers against his leg. It helped to center him and bring him back to the present. He once again slipped the stone away into his pocket. He'd keep it on him until he met up with Teryn. "On screen."

Sapere Mauktil, who had been talking to someone else in the room where he was, turned back toward his own video screen with a smile on his face. "On your way home, I see. How did your mission you go?"

"Without a hitch," Balthier answered, watching the sapere's face carefully for signs of displeasure.

"Good. And Moonhunter performed adequately?"

Balthier felt his facial muscles tightening and his lips barely seemed to move as he answered, "That he did."

"Good. Good." The sapere drew in a deep breath, one holding onto a lot of tension rather than releasing it. "I have been asked to get your thoughts on a subject regarding Moonhunter."

His awareness of the Onesong collapsed and Balthier hated that the mere mention of Moonhunter's name by a sapere caused him to shut down so quickly. "Regarding," Balthier snarled.

The sapere gave a soft smile. Balthier swore that in the training which saperes received, learning to smile just like this must be something they all received. Gentle, harmless, and yet somehow mocking all in one twist of the lips. Then the sapere answered in a tone which matched that taunting leer, "Why, Balthier, there is nothing you shouldn't be expecting. We were merely wondering if you felt that it was time for Moonhunter to stop being your apprentice and what your thoughts were in that regards."

Balthier hoped that the sapere's words hitting him in the stomach like a bucket of hot lava wasn't evident on his face. "Who specifically is asking: the saperes or the Dragon Council?"

Again, that smile meant to diffuse tension. "The saperes have been asked by the Dragon Council to assess Moonhunter's readiness. Is that not the way it generally happens?"

The boy is hiding something. The unbidden thought rose in Balthier's mind. What exactly was Moonhunter keeping from Balthier? Had Moon been contacted by the saperes too? Were they already in communication about removing Moon from his apprentice status?

Balthier let his finger flick the scrambler toggle on his control panel so that static flickered on the screen. He leaned forward and pretended to fix the situation so that it gave him a moment to let all the emotions snaking through him play out on his face. With a fist, he feigned banging it against the console. Then he flipped off the scrambler. "Sorry, Sapere. I must have hit some interference. Hopefully we are through it now. As for Moonhunter, the boy is skilled, but not tempered. He is addicted to speed and likes to do things fast. He tries to take shortcuts and is reckless."

The sapere leaned forward over the table holding his video panel and it made his face stretch across Balthier's screen a bit. "Sounds like a typical novihomidrak. But I suppose you are out in the field with him more than we are."

Nervous energy rolled through Balthier in a sick wave. "Just a little longer, Sapere. He's not quite ready yet, but he will be soon."

"All right. I will make that report. Thank you for your input. Maybe you would ask Moonhunter how he feels about taking the reins for himself. I suggest you use the time back on your trip to get a feel for where he feels he's at. Safe travels to you." The sapere's screen went blank.

Balthier leaned back in his chair, placed his hands on his face, and rubbed hard. He wasn't ready to let Moonhunter go. Not yet. Ideally, Moonhunter's last mission as an apprentice would also bring Balthier's death. He wasn't certain he wanted to live without Moonhunter as his student. For years, he'd searched for the reason behind Vehlka placing Moonhunter in his care, and the only thing he saw was that it had made him straighten out his life. Being on the straight and narrow for so long as he'd been, he didn't want to go back to the switchback curves he'd been able to put behind him.

He knew the saperes wouldn't care about that.

Sounds like a typical novihomidrak to me. The sapere's words mocked him. Moonhunter was more prepared to be a novihomidrak than Balthier. At least Moonhunter didn't have a death wish.

Did he really want to find out if Moonhunter was ready to stop being his apprentice?

No, not really. His heart might not be able to handle the answer.

"Rhonda, has Moonhunter logged into any onboard systems yet?"

"Negative." The computer paused as if it was capable

of thinking for a moment. "Would you like me to notify you when he does?"

"No." Balthier didn't want Moonhunter sensing something strange on the Humline, a little bump which would indicate that Balthier was wondering what Moon was doing. Best not to give any signs at all. He would just have to find out himself. Maybe it was time for them to have a talk.

As he stood up, the stone shifted in his pocket, reminding him that it was there. He pulled it out once more and stared at it, knowing it brought up more questions than answers.

He needed to speak with Moonhunter.

Much like he needed to see Teryn to find out why this little stone was so important.

On this mission, he seemed poised to lose more than he had gained.

4

The second Moonhunter heard Balthier's footsteps in the hallway, Moonhunter knew his time of patient meditation would soon end.

Balthier paced outside the door.

Just as Moonhunter was wondering why Balthier wouldn't make up his mind whether to enter or not, a heavy knock came to the door.

"There's a buzzer on the door. You could use that," Moonhunter called out. "Come in."

The door slid open and Balthier entered. He took a cursory look around, his gaze sweeping over Moonhunter sitting cross-legged in meditation on the bed. "For all the stars of the Onesong, don't tell me you're going all mental hoodoo on me."

"It's very calming. You should try it some time."

"We're novihomidraks. We're always tuned into the universe. You should already know that with all the crazy sh-tuff that goes on out there…"

Moonhunter smiled at Balthier catching himself.

"…we can't be calm. Ever."

"Call me when the ship… Rhonda… is in danger. Until then, I feel perfectly safe here and plan on continuing my meditation."

"Vehlka never told me you'd be a challenge."

"Do you need something?"

Balthier shuffled. Then he rubbed a hand over his beard, his fingers tugged down on it near the corners of his mouth. When he drew his hand away, he said, "I just wanted to let you know that we've left the planet without pursuit. Looks like we'll have a short, quiet flight back to Nevkor."

Moonhunter nodded.

Balthier glanced around again as if he were looking for something more in Moonhunter's room. Then he slapped his palms against the sides of his thighs and made to turn. "Well, I guess I'll let you get back to your meditation. Unless you want to join me up front for landing?"

"Afraid you can't land Rhonda yourself, old man?" Moonhunter joked, unable to resist doing so with Balthier's heavy mood. There was something that Balthier wasn't saying; what was the old man holding back? It wasn't like Balthier, who usually spoke his mind about everything.

"Ah, suit yourself. Stay here then."

"Don't worry about me. I'll just be here practicing my mental hoodoo."

Balthier left the room with a snort.

Moonhunter closed his eyes just in case Balthier re-entered, but the old man's steps faded toward the front of the ship. Probably going to go back to the flight cabin and kick back with his feet on the flight console. For some reason, Balthier felt more comfortable like that than in the cabin of his own. For such a short trip, he doubted that Balthier would go to his quarters at all.

Which meant Moonhunter had the back of the ship to himself.

With a grin, he jumped off the bed.

He hurried to the doorway and looked out just to make sure that Balthier had gone to deck and wasn't returning. After closing and sealing the door, Moonhunter removed his jacket and shirt. Let this not be the time that Balthier caught him.

His room had once been a cargo hold. At first, Moonhunter hadn't been happy with the conversion of his room, but now he saw why the Onesong had influenced Balthier to shift the cargo hold into housing quarters. Moonhunter retrieved four thick, black straps from a drawer near his bed and clicked the carabiner into the eyebolts placed in the ceiling. He doubted Balthier had ever questioned if these would be used for anything other than securing cargo, but Moonhunter had found them handy ever since his discovery.

He brought his hands up like claws in front of him, drawing air into his lungs as he gathered energy from the universe they were flying in. As his hands got higher, he spread them apart, imagining that they were giant wings unfurling. Once he could no longer take in air, he breathed out as hard as he could. The air was hot, not quite on fire, but enough for him to feel the rise in temperature. Sweat beaded over his tanned skin.

The small room grew warm enough that he knew he might not even feel the slight temperature change during re-entry. He grabbed onto two of the straps hanging from the ceiling and slid the loops around his wrists. He'd really like to be prepared by the time they started to descend toward Nevkor. His breath shortened and quickened as he felt his heart accelerate. This would be his first attempt at making it all the way to landing?

Last time, that hadn't gone so well.

"Turbulence," he whispered, "and Balthier's bad flying." Surely it didn't have anything to do with his own inexperience.

Moonhunter secured his grips on the straps, knowing this next step to be painful. "Rahh!" he screamed, tightening the muscles in his back as much as he could. Wings grew from his back.

Now for the hard part.

Sweat dripped down into his face as the wings began to beat. He felt his feet lift off the ground and in a moment they hit the ceiling.

Only here, in the lighter gravity made by the ship in space and with a heated room, had he ever been able to achieve flight. So far, his planet-based attempts hadn't worked. He twisted and tried to look for the loops at his feet. The first ankle was always the most difficult because he had nothing to put weight onto. Once he felt it and got his foot inside, he searched for the other loop.

His back pressed against the ceiling, his wings giving small flaps to keep him steady. He breathed more hot air into the room, feeling the heat gathering beneath his wings, which weren't quite strong enough to hold him aloft yet.

Which is why he spent every moment in space that he could to train. Had Balthier noticed the difference in him yet?

How would Balthier react to knowing Moonhunter had wings?

The saperes had told him that wings were a rarity. Only about one in every sixty or seventy.

Moonhunter exhaled another round of hot air into the room, letting his wings feel the lift it gave him. Then he stretched out his wings and gave a flap. The powerful stretch used every muscle along his back. He couldn't wait until he could actually do this without the use of the suspension straps.

Slowly, he tried to remind himself. He had to train his wings, abdomen, and legs. Having wings alone didn't assure flight. The human body wasn't designed for it and muscular development was a huge key to making it happen. But he wanted to do this himself. He didn't want Balthier's help. He wanted to surprise Balthier.

Besides, he wasn't certain Balthier wouldn't be jealous; wings were something Balthier didn't have. So it seemed even more important that Moonhunter train himself on his own and gain Balthier's approval in having done it right.

Moonhunter felt the ship start to descend. He couldn't believe they were reaching Nevkor already.

"Keep it steady, Balthier," he muttered, hoping that the energy would flow along the Onesong to Balthier.

Rhonda had good shields and airflow, but the ship still managed to gain a few degrees during re-entry into the atmosphere. Balthier had said that a woman working that hard deserved to sweat a little. No wonder Balthier had given the ship a feminine name. Of course, Balthier had made his statement in front of Sapere Lyma at the time. She swatted him, looking more like she really want to slap the novihomidrak, and informed Balthier that women didn't sweat; they perspired.

The thought of Lyma dragged Moonhunter's thoughts back to the saperes.

Only one in sixty or seventy novihomidraks had wings. If the saperes knew about his, would he be taken away from Balthier? Would he be sent to have more formal training with the saperes? Or would he be sent to live with one of the powerful members of the Dragon Council? His wings, even weak like they were, could change his life.

Another reason for him to keep them hidden.

And that was why no one must ever see him this way. Not until he was ready to inform Balthier.

The ship hit turbulence and he bounced against the ceiling of the craft. A small bone in his young wings cracked. Involuntarily, he yanked his hand out of the loop and reached for the injury. Skin like armor and bones like twigs. Something was wrong with the dragon's design!

More turbulence and Moonhunter hung from the three loops. He twisted his hand to grab the strap's material.

"Get it together, Balthier!" Moonhunter roared, his voice deeper, more guttural than normal.

His stomach lurched as he swung loosely from the loops again. His other hand slipped out of the loop and left him swinging upside-down. He tried to use his wings to stabilize himself, the broken bone protesting against the pull of still feeble muscles and tendons.

He reached up and grabbed the loops around his feet so he could pull himself free. Getting one foot out, another rocking bump made him lose his grip and left him swinging momentarily from one foot. It slipped from the loop, removing his boot as he fell. He landed fully on his back, crushing those poor wings beneath him.

At least he didn't feel them bend unnaturally.

He winced in pain as he sat up. His wings began to fold back under his skin.

Moonhunter grabbed his shirt and pulled it over his head. Already he felt the ship starting to settle. The shirt caught on a part of his still extended wing. The little bone wasn't letting it tuck in. He could feel it now: not only had the bone cracked with a hairline fracture, but it popped out of the joint. It felt like a little finger poking out near his shoulder blade.

Moonhunter growled as he reached back over his shoulder and touched the sensitive spot. It flared with pain, but at least it hadn't broken the skin. He'd gotten lucky this time. Trying to explain why he had venomcur poisoning from sitting on his bed in mediation would be hard to do. He could blame it on Balthier's lousy landing, but then Balthier would demand that Moonhunter drive and he'd never have time alone on the ship again. Still, Moonhunter doubted he could heal this alone.

He realized that he still needed to take down the straps. Reaching up to release the carabiner sent pain through his back and the part of the wing unable to tuck back in. Moonhunter didn't understand the anatomy of how it all worked other than that the bones shrunk in size to disappear under the skin in a similar way that the dragon teeth reverted back to the gums or their claws sunk into fingertips. As one sapere had put it so succinctly in his research into the dragon aspects: *novihomidraks are a weird species, their design flawed and concept nearly impossible. To imagine their existence, let alone their purpose, it is a wonder more of them are not crazy.*

Moonhunter hid the straps away and checked the mirror to see if the bone jutting out was noticeable. He couldn't completely tell.

Balthier would be here any moment to get him.

Moonhunter reached for his leather jacket. Maybe it would have enough bulk to the material that Balthier wouldn't notice. He'd just finished shoving his arm painfully down the sleeves when Balthier entered.

"Hey, champ, you make the landing?"

Moonhunter tried not to grimace. "Fine."

"That's all you can say for it? I made that landing smoother than a baby's behind."

"Who's using old clichés now?"

Balthier turned and started to walk out. "Hurry up. I want us to go tell the Council about this."

"Can't." Moonhunter rushed by Balthier, turning as he went by so that it looked like he was facing his mentor when really he was just trying to keep Balthier from seeing the jutting bone.

"Hot date?"

"Right. I'm meeting Serchk and we're heading over to the pools."

"If you spend half as much time training as you do swimming –"

"See ya!" Moonhunter turned and dashed away. He ran through the open door, jumping down before the landing crew even had the ramp up to the ship. He dashed through the landing bay, but hid quickly behind some crates. From the shadows, Moonhunter blinked his dragon lids into place and watched Balthier come down the ramp. Balthier took a quick look around without his dragon vision, shook his head, and started heading for the Council's offices. Breathing a sigh of relief, Moonhunter went the opposite direction toward the sanctuary. The sooner he found Serchk, the sooner he could fix what was broken.

F rom the outside, the soot-encrusted windows of the bar didn't look like they'd been cleaned in three years. Inside didn't look much better. Smoke hung in the air like the discordant twangs of the band tuning their instruments for this evening's entertaining. The floor's wooden slats creaked, giving way to the occasional crunch of a nutshell or two beneath Balthier's boots as he walked in.

A few of the tables were occupied, but hardly anyone looked up at the novihomidrak. Most people in here wanted to mind their own business, which suited everyone else just fine.

Balthier dropped down onto the stool at the counter and signaled the barkeep for a round. Getting a nod in response, Balthier turned to the man sitting beside him.

Teryn sighed as he glanced down at his drink and stirred the liquid inside the shot glass with a toothpick. "Aren't you a bit in a hurry today? Usually you let me move down the bar to you."

"Yeah, you always let me have a couple drinks first.

Here's the rub: it's always water they bring me. Alcohol and a Ch'bauldi novihomidrak's fire breath... generally not something that goes well together."

Teryn pulled the toothpick out and tapped it lightly against the glass a couple of times. "That's too bad." He set the slender wood on the counter, but let his finger linger on top of it to roll it back and forth. "I think I'd like to see you loosen up a little bit. Care to tell me what's got you in a hurry?"

The barkeep slid a glass in front of Balthier, nodded, and walked away.

Balthier took a hold of his newly arrived glass, but didn't lift it. "My apprentice kept saying that you had set us up. I just can't help but wonder if he was sensing something I might have been blind too."

Teryn turned his head to look fully at Balthier. The half of his face which had been away from Balthier revealed a mass of burns and scars which pulled down his left eye grotesquely. "Balthier, how long have we known each other?"

"Since you were a teen," Balthier answered, unable to take his eyes off the dark red flesh. A rush of memories overtook Balthier. He remembered creating those scars and searing burns. He'd thought the man was a novihomidrak.

"Had to put a lot of history behind us, haven't we?" he spoke followed by a low laugh.

Balthier wished Teryn wouldn't hold it over his head.

"When are you going to bring that adorable little apprentice of yours in here with you?" Teryn asked.

"When you feel like cleaning up your dealings," Balthier answered, turning on the stool to squarely face the counter and lean over it. He wished he'd not broken his normal routine and let Teryn get started.

"You don't think this arrangement works well between us?"

How was he supposed to reply? That he should have ripped Teryn's head clean off instead? Teryn had been trouble as a teen and it certainly hadn't gotten any better now as an adult.

Balthier decided not to answer. Instead, he fished in his pocket, pulled the stone out, and smacked it down on the counter. "Here's your worthless rock."

"Ah," Teryn said, reaching for it.

Balthier slammed his hand down on it, his claws extended for emphasis and digging just slightly into the wood. Let the marks be another permanent reminder to Teryn. "Why did you have me go and fetch this for you?"

"Don't tell me you're going to ask for a cut of the profits now."

"Wouldn't dream of it. Just want a reason." Balthier shrugged. "There's nothing special about this stone."

Teryn sighed. "That you are aware of." He gave an equally nonchalant shrug. "But it was special to someone, special enough that it was put into a museum."

"So?"

Teryn jerked his head. "So what?"

"So why was it put away? Come on, Teryn. Why would someone contact you to hire me to go get a simple rock? There's other mercenaries. You don't need a novihomidrak to be a thief unless there's a bigger reason."

Teryn's eyes widened and his mouth took on a round shape. "Ooh, you said it, not me. A novihomidrak thief." He clucked his tongue. "Is that a confession?"

Balthier grabbed the front of Teryn's shirt and dragged the man closer to him, near enough that the scent of alcohol bothered Balthier and he had to hold Teryn back a little.

Teryn took to his feet as he slid off the stool. "Why you little... if you are setting me up..." Balthier growled.

Teryn broke away and climbed back onto his stool. "Not you, Balthier."

"Moonhunter?"

"Ding, ding, ding. Give the man a prize."

"Leave Moonhunter out of this," Balthier warned. "Whatever they want with him, tell them to forget their plans now."

Teryn gave a mocking smile as he nodded. "Yeah, whatever."

Balthier grabbed Teryn's shirt again and dragged him even faster off the stool. He held Teryn in the air with both hands wrapped into the silk. "I swear, Teryn, I will rip your head off this time if anyone even thinks about a plot against Moonhunter."

Teryn seized Balthier's wrists as his feet flailed beneath him. "Okay, okay."

Balthier dropped Teryn, but didn't release his grip of the shirt.

"I think you need to quit playing this like you're a gangster," Teryn said, trying to pull away from Balthier.

"No, I leave that job to you, don't I? But I should be your worst fear."

Teryn stepped back from Balthier upon release and straightened his collar. "You know what your problem is, Balthier? You're too nice of a guy. Oh, yeah, you play tough, but deep down, you've got a guilt complex which keeps you from really going all dark." He pocketed the stone. "I just have to ask: did Moonhunter hold the stone?"

"What does it matter if Moonhunter touched it?"

"You're a novi, aren't you? You know how this works," Teryn mocked. "Touch a stone there, turn on a light somewhere else in the universe."

"Are you saying Moonhunter activated something?" Even while Balthier watched Teryn for signs of truth or a lie in the answer, he reached out to the Humline hoping to get his own insights.

"I'm just saying... I heard rumors."

"Rumors?"

"That Moonhunter is an innocent boy, isn't he? Or that's what you want everyone to believe. I heard from a space pirate that he might have killed a Necronosti." Teryn let silence fall as if he'd just turned over a handful of cards, letting everyone take in the royal flush before he started to collect the winnings. "Rumors, mind you."

"He was cleared of those charges." The words felt sticky in Balthier's throat.

"Yeah, but while he was stuck in probation while waiting for those proceedings, I heard that you ran a mission or two on your own, and those may have brought about some influences in your charge's favor. But these are just... rumors... unless you want to confess yourself right now."

"What is it that you want?"

Teryn shrugged and smiled. "Well, that sounds more like a bribe than a confession."

"It's neither. You're the one that's prodding and hoping to trip me up on something. Out with it."

Teryn's grin turned into more of a sneer. "I hear you knew the Necronosti... Verity, wasn't that her name... better than you told Moonhunter that you did. That's really why you knew she'd let you into her house. What would innocent Moonhunter think if he knew that you had once dabbled alongside Verity in the same dark arts, that you barely pulled yourself away from being a Necronosti yourself."

"Your rumors are just that."

"Balthier, a friendly word of advice… that light Moon-hunter turned on in the universe… make sure you're not a moth drawn to it. Aside from the possibility of getting burned, light has a way of exposing secrets, sometimes no matter how far in the shadows they are hidden."

"We're done here." Balthier rose.

"Yeah, don't worry. The saperes will pick up your bar tab just like they paid your landing and exit fees," Teryn announced as Balthier started to walk away.

"A sapere hired you to have me go after the stone?" Balthier slowly turned back toward Teryn.

"Oh, yeah, there it is. Guilt coming to eat at you again? Yeah, they know. More than one of them, Balthier. They've got all the proof they need against you now."

The mercenaries… Moonhunter had been right about there being a novihomidrak in their numbers. A sapere had sent someone to watch them.

"What do they want?" Balthier asked.

Teryn shrugged. "Don't know. Just did as they asked. I don't need trouble from saperes. Do you?"

"Yeah, I just might," Balthier said as he turned and walked out.

It gnawed at Balthier that Teryn had given him the information about Moonhunter and the saperes. Teryn wanted Balthier to know the details of the mission. What-ever Teryn had longed to say and couldn't, the particulars didn't sit well with Teryn.

That meant it was very bad.

Worse, now Balthier didn't know who to trust.

What was so important about that stone? Who wanted it and why? Did it have anything to do with the rock at all, or was it a test of Moonhunter's abilities?

Balthier started back for his ship. As he walked along the street, he pulled his tablet and punched in the code for his personal bank account. The monies due to him from Teryn had funneled in.

He paid half to Moonhunter's account. Then he transferred another half of the balance again. He knew he'd have to face Moonhunter's questions about that second movement of money, but that might be the easiest question he had to deal with. Now that Balthier knew that the job had come from a sapere and that it involved Moonhunter, he didn't feel right keeping any more of the money than a simple quarter share.

Of course, Moonhunter didn't realize that he was receiving this payment as funds for being a mercenary. He believed it merely his regular compensation from the saperes, possibly with a bonus for a job well done.

He hated lying to Moonhunter. Yet, it was the only way to keep Moon from learning about Teryn. Just thinking about the younger novihomidrak realizing Balthier's disgrace brought a tightness he didn't like to his chest.

He often thought that Vehlka had made a mistake in choosing Balthier as the mentor for her pevitias. Did she know about Balthier's past? Certainly, as his novimather, she must. Had it been her attempt at saving him too? Did Vehlka realize how close Balthier walked the line to succumbing to chaos and becoming a Necronosti? But with Moonhunter at his side, that time of his life felt further and further away.

Except for Teryn, the one entanglement that remained.

Balthier had to admit that Moonhunter had probably kept him from letting chaos into his heart. Surely Vehlka had known how close he was.

His anger grew as he walked along. He couldn't let the saperes do anything that might harm Moonhunter. Balthier bit back the growl he felt rising in his throat.

But his thoughts alone were enough to make Balthier sway from his path back to his ship to head toward the temple. Some sapere there knew something; one of them had hired Teryn, knowing Teryn would take the job to Balthier.

Rather than searching the Humline in solitude, he would discover who it was as he walked through the temple's halls.

The Wells help him if he discovered the Grand Sapere behind all of this.

The thought alone was enough to make his claws extend from beneath his fingernails and dig into his palms. The skin tightened, resisting, then gave way to the sharp points. Only when he picked up the scent of his own blood did he realize that in his irritation he had injured himself.

He stared in even greater annoyance at the blood seeping into his palms. Now he'd need a sapere to heal these too.

"Vehlka, why did you leave the boy to me?" he asked in a muttered tone.

The wind picked up through the trees and shook their leaves as if in answer to his question.

Once blood pooled enough to start dripping over the sides of Balthier's hands, he quit trying to hold them up and allowed them to leave a trail of red behind him.

"Balthier," a sapere in yellow and brown robes shouted at him upon seeing the injured novihomidrak enter the temple. "What happened to you?"

"Doesn't matter," Balthier growled. "Self-inflicted."

"Why did you do that to yourself?"

Balthier scanned the Grehhest sapere over. The Humline responded with the sapere's innocence. "Please find me a Ch'bauldi sapere."

The sapere nodded and ran off down the halls.

Balthier's hands ached up into his wrists, a sensation like worms twisting under his skin as the infliction worked its way through him. Figuring he should try to contain the blood from dripping all down the halls and making some poor soul, someone who wouldn't be a sapere, from having to clean up after him, Balthier wrapped his hands into the cloth of his shirt and made his way toward an unoccupied medical room.

Standing near the open window, Balthier heard Moonhunter's low, rumbling laugh. Balthier moved where he could see Moonhunter with his companions as they went through the courtyard. It seemed no coincidence that the Humline had led him here to watch proudly from a distance. He smiled to himself. Moonhunter was maturing so fast, even though he would continue to look like a boy for many more years. How much longer would Moonhunter need him?

How much longer would he need Moonhunter?

6

Moonhunter lay on his stomach, shirtless, with his head hanging over the edge of the bed. The cozy red and gold bed coverings were cool against his skin. He stared at the plush red carpet wondering if seeking his friend for a healing was a good idea, even though it had been his own.

His friend, Serchk, had wanted to take him to a higher ranked sapere for official medical attention. Moonhunter insisted this remain between them. Serchk's next option was for one of the medical rooms where Serchk would have supplies, but that could lead to questions if they were found in there. Both of Serchk's options were bad as far as Moonhunter was concerned. Yet lying here, with the heady frankincense still burning in the air, Moonhunter felt his world spinning. Or maybe the lingering energies from Serchk's meditation prickled at Moonhunter's senses. Or, maybe it had to do with his anger over the self-imposed pain he knew was coming.

"Ow!" Moonhunter said as the sapere touched the

protruding wing. "What part of 'it's jammed' didn't you understand?"

"Do you want this fixed or not?" Serchk responded. "Fortunately, you're wrong; it's not broken. I do think it's dislocated though. Can you extend the wings again?"

Moonhunter closed his eyes and focused. He felt the wings grow.

"I still don't believe you can do this," Serchk said. "I wish you'd let me tell the Grand Sapere."

"No. No one can know. Not until we're sure."

"You're growing wings. That's pretty certain."

"They are useless unless I can get strength into them," Moonhunter growled.

"Hold still." Serchk put his hands around the little bone. Moonhunter felt the sapere's warming hands take a grip on the wing. A second later, Serchk pulled.

Moonhunter jumped to his feet and spun around. The length of his wing yanked from Serchk's hands. "That hurt." Once again, his voice had deepened and he felt like burning his friend in terrible fire.

Serchk dropped to the ground, bowing his head to the carpet. "Forgive me."

The reverence made Moonhunter calm down almost instantly. Saperes should always bow down before the novi-homidraks.

Wouldn't Balthier love to hear him say that? Moonhunter chuckled to himself, shaking both thoughts out of his head before reaching down for Serchk to help the sapere get up. Once Serchk was on his feet, Moonhunter found himself unable to look at the sapere standing before him. "I don't know if the strength training for my wing is working. I'm afraid it's getting worse."

"Will you let me look at your wing again?"

Moonhunter nodded. "Maybe I should remain standing?"

Serchk gave a nervous laugh. "So you could just spin around and slash my throat open. No, thank you. If we went to a medical room, I could chain you down," Serchk said with a shake of fear still in his voice.

"Fine, I'll lie down again. I don't think we need to go that far." Moonhunter stretched out on the bed, the blankets refreshed with their chill beneath his bare skin. Once again, he stared at the red carpet and thought about how it was an improvement over the wood slats of the floor where Serchk had been as a trainee.

Serchk's hands felt over his back. "You'll need to extend them again, but since you could retract it all the way let's hope we got the bone back in its joint."

Moonhunter hadn't even realized that he'd pulled his wings in. He felt them slide over his back.

"I can't tell you how cool that is," Serchk said as he began manipulating the wing.

"What color are they? Do they have any markings yet?"

"They are Ch'bauldi red," Serchk responded with reverence. "Each scale is tinged with gold. It's like looking at the sun. No markings yet."

Moonhunter heard Serchk move aside, but he remained with the image Serchk had painted in his mind of his wings and tried to imagine flying. A flowery scent came to him and Moonhunter wondered if Serchk had gone to switch incense.

Hands were on Moonhunter's wings again. Warmth seeped into him at the soft touch and gentle probing.

"I told Balthier that we were going to the pools. After this, you can get away, right?" Moonhunter asked.

"That depends on who you're asking."

At the sound of a female voice, Moonhunter rolled and fell off the bed. Laughter followed his catastrophic shock as he fell to the carpeted floor, realizing that it had been Sapere Sundancer who'd had her hands on his wing.

"I'm sorry," Serchk pleaded. "She made me."

Sundancer leaned over the bed, her red and gold dress dipping low while her blue eyes twinkled with mischief. "I did. Anything to see Moonhunter without his shirt."

His shirt! He reached up to where he'd left it on the bed and gave it a yank. She'd put her elbow down on it, so the material resisted and stretched, then snapped from beneath her. He gathered the material over his chest.

"Wings, huh?" she asked. "Anything else about you I should know? Other enhanced parts?"

"Uh, no!" Moonhunter jumped to his feet and turned away while he pulled his shirt on. His wings hadn't retracted yet. In fact, they stood straight out to the sides as if they'd been scared stiff.

Sundancer laughed at him. He continued to struggle to pull his shirt down over his chest even if he couldn't get it over his back.

Heat rose in his throat and he spun away. "This is too dangerous!" He barely got the last word out before he felt a roll of vomit rising in his throat. No, it wasn't bile. He tried to swallow it back, but it was so hot. Steam spilled out between his grit teeth.

"He's smoking," Sundancer hollered.

Moonhunter heard her steps rush forward. He looked over his shoulder to see Serchk grab Sundancer's arm as she started toward Moonhunter.

"Stay back," Serchk warned. "It's his dragon breath."

"Dragon breath," she whispered, but in Moonhunter's ears it sounded like a loud siren.

It wouldn't tame back down. He had to open his

mouth and let it out. So he did, much like he had on the ship, and only a ball of hot air came out. Without windows, the room heated and Moonhunter watched as Serchk and Sundancer began to sweat.

"There was no fire," she said, sounding disappointed.

Moonhunter's throat felt raw. He clasped onto it as if his hands could heal it. He'd never fought the dragon breath before. Had he burned the inside? Either way, he couldn't speak up to defend himself.

Fortunately, Serchk jumped in to explain. "He hasn't been able to produce fire yet. But he's only just started working at the dragon breath."

Her eyes widened. "You guys really are doing the Crossover and it's working." Her mouth parted as she stared between the two of them. She walked over to Moonhunter.

He couldn't move. The sound of her slippers grew louder as she got closer, not to mention the faint rustle of her sapere dress as she moved. The shirt slid down on his back letting him know that his wings had retracted. It settled into place as she reached him.

"You can blink the dragon lids away now," Sundancer said. "You're not in danger from me."

He hadn't even realized that his dragon lids had come down, sharpening his vision as well as his other senses. One didn't need the Crossover ceremonies to have that dragon ability. All novihomidraks had the dragon vision. In recent centuries, the council had deemed the other dragon abilities as unnecessary and had stopped the Crossover ceremonies, but Moonhunter knew if the vision was powerful, how much more formidable would the Crossover make him? He blinked and his normal sight returned.

"So what happened to your wing?" Sundancer asked, reaching out to touch his shoulder.

"They're brittle," Serchk responded for him. On the one hand, Moonhunter was glad because he wasn't sure he could speak with his sore throat, and angry because Serchk had shown her a weakness in him. The sapere continued, "We're hoping it's just because the wings are immature. But he is getting started a couple years late, so there's a possibility they won't develop correctly. We also have to consider that his mother died shortly after birthing him; she barely lived through his naming. He can no longer draw on her power to help him. There are so many factors to bear in mind."

Moonhunter held up his hands and stared at Serchk as if saying, "What the hell? Confess much?" but without the actual words.

Serchk blushed.

Sundancer was now walking around Moonhunter. "That could be the reason why his fire breath isn't coming in either. All those very reasons."

"Exactly. We don't know, but we keep working at it. We won't get anywhere if we don't' try."

Moonhunter wished his voice had come back to him, but it still hurt too much. Serchk just wasn't taking the hint to shut up. Everyone who knew that Moonhunter was attempting the Crossover was one more person who could be a liability. Didn't Serchk understand that? That had been precisely why he couldn't have anyone other than Serchk, who had known about Moonhunter working at the Crossover for several months now, look at the damage he'd done to his wing.

"I want to help," Sundancer stated.

Serchk looked scared. "What we're doing isn't exactly illegal, but it isn't authorized either. The council doesn't know."

"Which is one of the very reasons I can, and should,

help. With my father on the council, I can make sure that your experiment stays silent. I mean, I will know if they even start to suspect and consider putting together a committee to look into it." She looked at Moonhunter. "Or, if you guys are discovered, I might be how we get the council to give leniency in any punishment they might dole out."

It seemed solid, these reasons of hers.

"You'll also need a female sapere if you plan on finishing the Crossover," she said, now putting a hand on her hip as if the action indicated a final nail in her argument. She smiled.

She certainly wasn't wrong there. Serchk shrugged as if letting Moonhunter know the decision was his. Of course, he was the one performing the Crossover after all; it was his body he was manipulating. He wished he could say he was perfecting it, enhancing the gifts given to him when he awoke as a novihomidrak, but he was beginning to have his doubts. None of this was reversible. If he screwed it up... Did he want his shame to be seen by someone else? Yet, she was also right, and he and Serchk had talked a few times about how to handle the ceremonies without the necessary saperes. They weren't sure it was possible and had decided to see what would come. Now, here was Sundancer, beautiful and willing to help him.

Why? The other side of his mind suddenly questioned her actions. Why would she help him? What was she getting out of this? She had to know that Moonhunter had a crush on her; who didn't? If they were successful at this, yes, they would probably be hailed as heroes. But if they failed, he would end up ugly and disfigured, not exactly something anyone would want to be around. He would either be the pinnacle of the novihomidraks or a cripple. It could go either way. Why would she want to align herself with those possibilities?

"Fine," Moonhunter said, his voice like a deep croak. He could agree now, settle the problem for the moment, and talk her out of it later… when he could actually speak.

"Spectacular!" She spun around on her slippered foot. "Shall we all head down to the pools now and discuss where you guys are at and what we do next?"

They rushed from the room, nearly colliding with someone walking in the hallway. The saperes all muttered quick apologies to each other, then they went about their ways.

"Where are you three off to in such a hurry?" a nearby sapere asked after watching them. He stepped toward them as he spoke.

Both Serchk and Sundancer bowed to Sapere Mauktil while Moonhunter remained tall, though silently wondering why the sapere had to be so nosey.

"We're off to the pools," Sundancer commented. "Trying to give Moonhunter a bit of relaxation before heading out on another mission."

Two thoughts hit Moonhunter simultaneously: was Mauktil coming to tell Moonhunter he had another mission, and why did Sundancer have to sound so happily innocent?

Mauktil glanced between Serchk and Sundancer. "You two have both finished your studies for the day."

Sundancer looked as she might pirouette as she clasped her hands in front of her and nodded. Serchk, on the other hand, put on a covering smile. "I will, Sapere. I am nearly there. Moonhunter is rarely here, and certainly not for long."

"See that you don't let visiting your friend keep you from getting to your studies."

Serchk started to answer, but another sapere rushed over to speak with Mauktil. His mouth opened as his gaze shifted to Moonhunter, then he stretched up on his toes and cupped his hand as he whispered in Mauktil's ear.

Moonhunter listened. All he picked up was Balthier's name along with the word healing.

Mauktil nodded to the sapere, who then went rushing off. Mauktil smiled. "If you all will excuse me now, there is a matter I must attend to."

Moonhunter grabbed Mauktil's red sleeve. "Is it Balthier? Is he injured?"

The sapere patted Moonhunter's hand. "I assure you he is in no danger. Only a minor mishap. Please, continue to enjoy the company of your friends. I must return."

Moonhunter didn't release him yet. "But why the need for secrecy if it was nothing?"

Mauktil gave a gentle smile. "You know Balthier's pride."

The subtle warning to not embarrass Balthier knotted on Mauktil's words. Moonhunter let the sapere go, watching the man breeze off.

"Come on," Serchk said, knocking Moonhunter's arm. "Let's go."

Moonhunter took a second as he turned to feel along the Humline for any danger surrounding Balthier. When none came back to him, he released his worry and followed his friends.

7

Balthier heard shuffling steps behind him as someone entered the medical room. He turned, pleasantly surprised to see Sapere Mauktil in his red and gold robes coming toward him.

"Balthier, I hear you're injured," Mauktil said.

Balthier held up the hand he'd wrapped in his brown shirt.

Mauktil's eyes widened as he saw the blood seeping up the fabric and darkening it. "Self-inflicted, I hear."

Balthier lingered by the door, listening for footsteps in the hallway, then drew it shut. "Miex'calidori," he said, just to make sure someone on the other side of the door wouldn't hear their conversation inside.

"Self-inflicted in anger, I see," Mauktil remarked.

The gnawing, twisting feeling had reached Balthier's elbows now. He swore he could feel every muscle and tendon in his forearms. "You're the only sapere I completely trust."

Mauktil's eyes reflected amusement but said nothing, clearly humoring Balthier's statement. He motioned

Balthier over to the table rather than the reclining vinyl chair and gestured for Balthier to take a seat on the stool across from him.

Balthier sat and placed his hands palms up on the red cloth covering the table. He slowly opened his fingers. Blood dribbled over the pinky sides of his hands.

With some gauze, Mauktil dabbed at soaking up the blood from the skin until he could see the wounds more clearly. He leaned in close to examine them. "It looks like your claws did this. Clenched your fist too tightly did you? Did it prevent you from ripping someone's head off?"

"It did."

"But did it get you anywhere other than here needing the healing of a sapere?"

"No."

"That's a shame. I would have hoped that it would teach you a lesson as well." Mauktil picked up a clean gauze strip and moistened it with rubbing alcohol.

"Damn the Ch'bauldi and their sense of nobility and honor. This wouldn't be happening if I'd been swallowed by any other dragon."

"A Shil'mak dragon, perhaps?"

Balthier issued an irked scoff.

"Be as angry as you want, Balthier, but you know Vehlka chose you and she did so because she knew your heart would hold the valor that it does."

"Valor," Balthier sneered again.

"Does it not take strength and courage to endure what you have gone through?" Mauktil dabbed gently to clean the wounds.

Growling, Balthier jerked his hand away, got up, and went to the sink where he began to wash his hands under the faucet. The dark red blood thinned in the water and swirled in bright crimson down the drain. Crimson droplets continued to bead on his skin from the punctures, so he didn't want to pick up one of the fresh towels. Instead, he blew a stream of hot air over his palms. Slamming himself back down on the stool, he smacked his arms on the table. "I'm not a daisy and I'd like to meet the germ that would like to kill me," he growled at Mauktil.

"No, instead you would prefer going the way of novi-homidrak self-poisoning." Mauktil's smile remained. "The novihomidrak's way is one of charging, but the sapere's path is dedicated to patience."

"Is that what you're doing now? Having patience until I explain what happened?"

Mauktil's smile broadened. "That would be you charging ahead, assuming the intentions of everyone around you. You may start whenever you wish."

Balthier hated that Mauktil had made an invitation out of his annoyance.

The sapere returned to the task of cleaning the wounds. "You might be immune to germs, but it is funny what can still get under our skin and fester." He paused as if making sure that Balthier understood the double meaning of his words. "No, you wouldn't want me to have to reopen a wound, would you?"

Balthier snarled and looked away.

"Sorry if that stung," Mauktil said, drawing back.

"Only the bite of your words, not the cleaning."

Mauktil began a low chant akin to a lullaby, yet the sound of it smashed against Balthier like tall crashing waves upon rocks.

"Steady," Mauktil uttered between verses of the dragon language that would nullify the poisonous venomcur making its way up Balthier's arms and healing the wounds.

Balthier wanted to curl his fingers back over his palms,

but Mauktil pressed them down. "You probably should have locked me in the chair," Balthier warned.

"Much like you trust me as a sapere, I have faith in you."

A tremble went through Balthier and then the sapere's words broke him. "I think Moonhunter is in danger."

Mauktil scoffed. "The boy thought *you* might be in danger when I was sent for to treat your wounds."

Balthier felt worry clench his brow. "Does that mean he knows something is wrong?"

"No. He was only worried."

"But he still sensed something. Damn." Balthier glanced away as Mauktil continued his chant of healing dragon magic. "Do you have any information?"

The soft, flowing song broke as Mauktil turned his gaze up to from the wound to look at Balthier. "The novihomidrak charging in for information now. Do you really have no patience at all, Balthier?"

The aching had nearly completely eased from Balthier's arms. Only faint traces of the sharpness remained in his wrists. "Vehlka charged me with taking care of Moonhunter. He's her pevitias. When I accepted, it was arrogant of me to think I was anywhere close to handling it. I should have known that I wasn't good enough for him or the position."

"Everyone makes mistakes," the sapere said in a soothing tone not too different than the dragon magic he spoke. He continued the tune for a moment longer before adding, "Even novihomidraks are not exempt from sometimes taking wrong paths."

"But we should know better. Our connection to the Onesong should keep us from straying."

"Maybe the Onesong would mean for you to stray. It works in mysterious ways."

"Then there would be no such things as mistakes," Balthier retorted sharply.

"Exactly my point."

Did Mauktil not realize that he had just contradicted himself? But as Balthier pondered over the question, Mauktil raised his gaze which hid a coy smile beneath.

"You are allowed to have your past, Balthier, and you have done what you could to make sure Moonhunter avoided those same trails you found yourself on. You walked down them and saw they lead nowhere good, so you averted Moonhunter from them. Would that not make you a wise mentor for Vehlka's pevitias?" Again he paused, whispering additional chants while he let Balthier stew on his words. "In hindsight, there are no mistakes."

"This is why I hate you saperes. Your words are always a preachy trap."

"The whispers of the Onesong come from many directions in our lives. Sometimes they are a feeling, or the little voice in your head. Other times, they can be as direct as a sapere's preachy words. Are you listening now, novihomidrak?"

"I am listening for you to give me my answer, sapere. I have yet to get any substantial reply to my question, and, as you said, novihomidraks are not known for our patience."

Mauktil soaked a new piece of gauze and dabbed against at the skin healing on Balthier's palms. "I don't even think it'll leave a scar. I do good work."

"Is there something that the saperes want from Moonhunter," Balthier pressed, sounding just a little harder, his voice intentionally a little deeper.

Mauktil's eyebrows raised. "The saperes always want our novihomidraks to be healthy and fit for their duties. It is why the dragons created us, and why you need us. To watch over you."

"Moonhunter is fit and healthy. What do the saperes want from him?"

Mauktil gathered the supplies he'd used and tossed them in a nearby garbage can. He started to rise. Balthier stood before him and blocked the sapere's path.

"I grow tired of asking. Do not make yourself one of the saperes I distrust."

All of the typical humor Mauktil's face normally held shattered as he dropped the guise. "Balthier, I do not believe you fully trust me either. I would like to think that you do, but I suspect we both know that is impossible. As for Moonhunter, you said it yourself: he is a pevitias."

It suddenly struck Balthier that a novihomidrak of a pevitias might have some significance to the saperes. The image of the saperes surrounding Moonhunter came to him, but whether it was to worship the boy or to sacrifice him, Balthier couldn't decipher.

"What is going to happen to him?" Balthier asked. Now that the Onesong had shown him the image, he knew it would come to pass.

"He touched the stone?"

It took Balthier a moment to realize that Mauktil meant the stone he had just given to Teryn. "Yes."

"Then the Onesong is expecting him. He will be sent to Vergnamet 3."

Sickness rolled through Balthier. "That's the world in a galaxy currently colliding with its neighboring galaxy. I was supposed to get Dr. Melstone from there and I failed."

"The Council is preparing to give him the order."

"Why would they send Moon there?"

Mauktil's gaze dropped to the floor as he inhaled a deep breath through his mouth, which he then rapidly closed. Balthier realized that the gesture symbolically meant Mauktil was not going to answer the question. At least not without some encouragement.

Balthier's voice dropped. "Tell me why Moonhunter is being sent to that world." Even he felt the rumble in the command echo off the walls around him.

Mauktil looked about to speak, but then he roughly shook his head. "Don't you try to dragon magic me," Mauktil warned, his usually warm eyes narrowing. "I will continue to resist it."

Feeling his chest inflate with more air, Balthier once again let the order shake from him, this time in the dragon language which he knew the sapere would understand perfectly well.

Mauktil grimaced, then snarled. "Damn you, Balthier!"

All the anger sapped out of Balthier as if draining out to his feet. His shoulders slumped. "Come on, Mauktil. Give me something."

For a moment, it looked like Mauktil might deny him. Then, breaking the clench of his pursed mouth, he said, "Moonhunter was slated to go alone, since the trip through the Wells will be dangerous. I will see what I can do with the Dragon Council. It would have been easier if you hadn't failed the first time."

"Then tell them I found out about Moonhunter being sent and told you he wasn't ready. Tell them that I want to make amends."

"I will. We already believe extraction of the scientist will be easier; the Council has approved removal of his family as well."

At least that was some good news.

"So, what makes this scientist so special and why send Moon to get him?" Balthier asked, wondering how much more information he could get out of Mauktil now that the pump had been primed.

"The two are not related."

Mauktil's flat words ran tremors up Balthier.

"Why not?" Balthier asked as tingles assaulted the back of his arms and legs. His rising hair made him want to snarl. It felt like electricity gathering around him, warning him not to proceed. "What is on that planet?"

Mauktil slowly shook his head. "Something only a pevitias should ever know about." He tried to force his usual smile back onto his face, his cheeks pressing up against his eyes. "I wish I knew that you would believe me when I say it's really a good thing for Moonhunter."

It rather felt like a door being slammed in his face. "Why keep a good thing secret?"

Now Mauktil's smile did become genuine as he lightly answered, "The same reason you trust no sapere. Trust can be dangerous."

"Is he going to be hurt?" All the vibrations now seemed to center in Balthier's chest. "I made a promise to Vehlka."

Mauktil reached out and grasped Balthier's arm in a friendly manner as he stepped around and started for the door. "Your promise to Moonhunter will remain intact. I will see what I can do about getting you to go with him. I will let you know what the Dragon Council says and inform you when you are to leave. In the meanwhile, don't injure yourself without cause again, please."

Balthier watched the sapere's back as Mauktil walked down the hall until he turned a corner out of sight. Something about this still didn't feel right. He looked down at his palms, healed, but there was something written across his skin in reddish-gold. He recognized the Ch'bauldi dragon scrawl. One sentence on each hand and beginning to fade fast.

Trust.

No one.

As soon as he had read it, the dragon writing vanished in little red and gold sparkles rising off his flesh.

8

The pools of Calrek were said to have been formed
from the bones of a giant after the Ch'bauldi
dragons killed him. The cave sheltering the
mineral water bathes were supposedly the giant's chest and
the tunnels leading to them were the inside of the bones of
his arms. Moonhunter had always thought the myth a bit
too much because the cave looked nothing like the inside
of a chest. It made more sense that this was all from
volcanic activity that had taken place centuries ago.

Myths were never logical. Yet, there was always some
truth to them. Chances were that these caves were once
where a Ch'bauldi dragon had taken on a giant of some
sort. He liked to imagine that it was a frost giant trying to
come through from Jotunheim and the dragon had burned
it until it melted and made the pools in here. Since the
water was always fresh and clean though, he logically knew
a supply of water had to be coming from an aquifer inside
the lava tubes.

He still liked his story better.

If only the walls could speak and tell him what had happened here.

The cave walls sparkled in the light of their lanterns as Moonhunter, Serchk, and Sundancer walked as little chips of granite glistened in the rock.

"Moonhunter! Earth to Moonhunter," Serchk called out to him. "Are you getting lost again?"

"Probably dreaming about science again," Sundancer laughed.

Moonhunter felt encouraged at her mocking. There was such a daring to it. He had this image in his mind of jumping from one space dock platform to another. That same kind of daring surged through him now. "Ah, come on guys, you can't tell me that you don't find this fascinating. Don't you ever wonder—"

"No," Serchk answered dryly. "I don't look the walls when I come here. I look at that." Serchk came up behind Moonhunter and turned Moonhunter's head to look at a girl in a form-fitting swimsuit. "Now that's fascinating!"

Serchk practically dropped all his belongings on the rock floor, swept clean, and dashed for the pools. He gave a yell as he jumped in front of the girl. Thank goodness Serchk was underwater and missed her sharply chiding remarks. They were not kind. She apparently had come here to be seen and not splashed.

Moonhunter heard Sundancer untying the knot on her robe and the material slipping from her shoulders. He glanced in her direction, his heart stopping when he saw her. She also wore a tight swimsuit, but the straps of this one were thinner than the other girl's. A diamond shaped pattern cut from just below her breasts down to passed her navel. He'd seen other women on lots of other planets with skin exposed, the universe's oldest profession alive and well throughout the galaxy, but to see Sundancer made his blood heat.

He tore his gaze away before she noticed. She was going to help him with the transforming. He couldn't get involved.

His body already was.

He wanted to growl, to roar. Suddenly he was all too aware of the steam in here. It felt so hot.

"Moonhunter," Sundancer said, slightly ahead of him, "are you coming?" Beyond her, Serchk pushed himself from the pool, seeming to ignore the girl he'd previously been trying to impress.

Moonhunter had a vague awareness that Serchk was moving toward him. He wanted to lash out, to bite. He curled his fingers into fists as if the action would will strength back into him. Instead, he felt his nails extending and cutting into his palms. He heard bare feet moving toward him, water dripping, heartbeats quickening.

Sundancer stepped in front of him. "Your eyes are red. Why do you have your dragon lids down?"

Serchk gasped as he pushed Sundancer aside. "Moon, don't go all werewolf on me now. Come on back."

"I'm trying," Moonhunter snarled.

"Try harder, man. People are starting to stare."

"Is this supposed to be happening?" Moonhunter asked, finding his voice almost a deep growl. "Is this normal?"

"There's a reason novihomidraks stopped trying to do the Crossing." Serchk's own voice was low with anger. "You wouldn't listen to me when I tried to tell you that. This is dangerous and the results unpredictable."

"I have to get stronger," Moonhunter said, pleading with his friend to understand, but how could Serchk when he barely understood this need himself. It just was this instinct that gnawed at him and burrowed deep inside him to his bones. He had to be faster, better… to shape himself as the best novihomidrak he could be as if all of the other novihomidraks were depending on it. It was his duty, this calling, and he had to heed. But he wasn't getting there fast enough.

He needed to be alone, to practice some more. He didn't have time for this leisurely distraction. Coming to the pools with his friends had been a mistake.

"I'm sorry, guys." Moonhunter pulled his towel over his head as he turned and started back toward the cave's entrance. He hoped that under the darkness of his makeshift cloak, his eyes weren't glowing. He felt Serchk and Sundancer at his heels and thought he heard their protests, but the noise might have been from the sound of the blood pounding in his ears.

He ran away just a touch faster, getting out of the tunnels before they could catch up to him.

Moonhunter was back out into the sunlight and cool air when he saw Balthier enter the courtyard. The sight of his mentor made everything inside him stop all at once. All the instincts he'd been feeling literally only moments before vanished in a wisp.

He suddenly felt ordinary and a little dead inside.

Balthier looked Moonhunter over as he finished crossing the grass, then nodded. "Hope you're done relaxing. Council says we're up again."

Serchk hadn't given up the chase and caught up with Moonhunter. He put his hand on the novihomidrak's shoulder. "We just got here," Serchk complained. Then, seeming to remember that it looked like they were leaving, finished with, "Moonhunter just forgot to take a pee before we went in."

Moonhunter turned and gave Serchk a what-the-hell

look. Serchk shrugged. "Isn't this mission something you could handle yourself?" Moonhunter asked. He felt an edge on the Humline that he really wouldn't approve of this mission. "I'd really like to rest and take a break, relax some."

Balthier looked less than impressed. "Duty calls."

The words were so flat, a tone reserved for putting an end to any argument Moonhunter could possibly make.

Balthier left and Moonhunter followed. He handed his towel back to Serchk and didn't even look at Sundancer as he continued after Balthier. How much more could he embarrass himself in front of her today? Maybe it was best that he did leave.

"No rest for the wicked, eh, Moon?" Balthier said finally as they left Serchk and Sundancer far behind. "I figured we'd be good for a week off. 'Parently not."

"What are we doing this time?" Moonhunter wasn't certain he was ready to fly out again. But the sight of the pistol and dagger on Balthier's belt said there might be more to this mission than he'd been currently told.

"We're going out-solar this time."

"Out-solar?" Moonhunter felt the excitement sprout inside him. If he had his choice between off-world missions and out-of-solar-system ones, he'd pick out-solar every time. He loved going to another galaxy and looking up at the stars on the world in which they landed, wondering if somewhere out there he stared up at his own galaxy. "Have we been there before?"

"You haven't."

It's not like Balthier ever said much, but there was something in his clipped words that was stranger than usual. Moonhunter looked at Balthier, who instantly cracked under the look. His shoulders sagged as he gave a defeated shake of his head. Seeing Balthier cave like that scared Moonhunter.

"We're going to clean up one of my messes."

"Oh," Moonhunter said. He looked down at the ground as he walked along, the oppressive seriousness of the situation deepening and weighing down on him. What more was he supposed to say to that? A novihomidrak wasn't supposed to mess up a mission to the point it was deemed a failure. Due to the very nature of the novihomidraks, it didn't often happen. It wasn't like Balthier was always perfect, but Moonhunter knew that Balthier didn't often make mistakes of a cataclysmic proportion. No wonder Balthier sounded abrupt.

"What can you tell me about Vergnamet 3?"

"Vergnamet 3?" Moonhunter asked again as if he hadn't quite heard Balthier correctly. He knew by the look in the older man's eyes that it was right. Vergnamet 3. Moonhunter listened with his mind for a hum he knew throughout the universe. When he felt it and could just barely hear it, he grabbed a hold of it mentally and felt its power move through him. "Vergnamet 3 is the third planet in the Vergnamet system and is one of two designated with life, the other being Vergnamet 5. The galaxy which holds the Vergnamet system is currently colliding with its neighboring galaxy." As he received this information from the Humline, Moonhunter broke away. "We're going to a galaxy which is currently colliding with another one?"

"You've been practicing," Balthier said proudly. Moonhunter thought he actually saw the old man smile. "And yes, that's exactly what we're doing."

"There might be cracks in the Wells. This is insane! You realize we could get lost, separated, or worse."

Balthier laughed. "I see now why Vehlka gave you Serenity and Tranquility."

At the mention of his dagger and bow, Moonhunter realized he'd need them for the mission. If they were going to a world… no, a whole galaxy currently being destroyed, he'd need them now rather than when he got there. If the Wells were half annihilated, he wanted them with him before going in. Afterward, there would be no guarantee that his weapons would make it to him. The point taken, Moonhunter whispered, "Vochey," and his weapons appeared on him. He felt the weight of Serenity, his dagger, come into the once empty sheath at his side as if it had sneaked out for an adventure and was now coming home. His bow, Tranquility, manifested on its strap, which held it and the quiver of arrows on his back. As it settled, he felt it rub against an area of skin still raw from healing from his incident with the dragon wings. He didn't utter a word of complaint; he couldn't have Balthier questioning him about what was wrong. Not that it mattered too much. Having his weapons settle in with him instantly brought a flood of soothing emotions to him. Every time he called his weapons back, he realized that he'd missed them terribly.

"So why do we have to go clean up your mess on a planet which is about to be torn to shreds?" Moonhunter asked. "Does it really even matter?"

"Yeah, it does." Balthier's tightened lips pulled into a deep frown. His steps got just a touch harder and faster, like he really wanted to storm and rage with his march. But he added nothing further to his words.

"Still got to pee?" Balthier asked. When Moonhunter shook his head, a look flashed across Balthier's face as if he'd always suspected Serchk's statement had been dubious. Then again, Balthier rarely trusted anything a sapere said to him.

They rounded the street corner and came into the council district. Large, white, marble buildings sported triangular roofs and striated columns. Moonhunter remembered thinking when he'd first seen this area that it looked like the Roman and Greek buildings of old back on Earth. He'd never actually seen the buildings because the planet had been lost first by the dragons, then by the unicorns, long before he'd become a novihomidrak. But he'd seen pictures in books salvaged by the handful of people the dragons had managed to save before earth's total destruction.

A sapere in a loose, red tunic wrapped with a golden belt ran over to them, slowing before intercepting them, and then bending over and placing his hands on his knees so he could pant. As Balthier approached, the man held up a piece of paper. "The coordinates are confirmed," the sapere said.

Balthier took the note. "Is it true the council approved his family this time? We won't go on this quest again if his family is to remain behind."

"The council approved," but the sapere's tone indicated that there was something about this decision they didn't like. What had put the council under such duress that they would overturn one of their own earlier decisions?

Balthier unfolded the papers, glanced it over, then passed it over to Moonhunter, who took it and read it.

"This puts us awfully near the center," Moonhunter said, as if unsure that these directions were true.

The sapere, still trying to catch his breath, fell into step beside them. "It's a galaxy in cataclysm. Through the dark is the only way. We do have a dragon guide for you."

"A Ch'bauldi I hope," Balthier said quickly.

"Sorry. The Ch'bauldi are too big to fit through some of the collapsed areas."

"And the Council doesn't want to risk the life of a

Ch'bauldi," Balthier finished the statement for the sapere; they all knew the truth, but only he was willing to say it.

The sapere huffed as he opened and closed his mouth. It was all the confirmation Moonhunter needed to know that Balthier was correct. "It's an extended branch. It gets awfully narrow from the gravitational imbalances."

"Rest it, sapere. Just tell me what dragon I should be expecting."

The sapere ran his fingers along the split neckline of his tunic. "Your guide is to be a Shil'mak."

Balthier stopped, his feet sliding on the pavement. His mouth dropped open and it was a moment before he could speak. "You have got to be kidding me. A Shil'mak?"

"She's small enough to fit through the collapsed branch and your best shot at making it there and back."

"You do realize that Moonhunter and I are both novi-homidraks of the Ch'bauldi dragons, right?"

The sapere nervously licked his lips. "Yes, I do."

"But you'll send us down a black Well with a Shil'mak?"

The sapere glanced down at the ground and took a deep breath. "She's the only… " Then he looked up at Balthier with sharp, angry eyes. "Would you rather that I request a Nefterru? I'd be glad to find you the meanest, orneriest one I can! Maybe the two of you would get along well."

Balthier started to laugh. "You saperes love your dragons too much."

"And you novihomidraks are arrogant son-of-a-bitches."

Moonhunter wondered what Balthier had seen on the sapere and he glanced the man over again, looking for the clue that would make this conversation have some sense to it. What had he missed? Then he noticed it, the little tattoo on the side of the sapere's ear written as a simple inscription: *Roc'ta-vay gilish Shil'mak*. I listen to the words of the Shil'mak. More and more, the dragon saperes were becoming generalists. Very few specialized in just one dragon clans' rituals any more. A changing time, brought on by dragons crossing clan lines to mate with other dragons.

"You make demands of the Dragon Council, push them into decisions they don't want to make, all because you can't complete your mission otherwise," the sapere pressed on.

Balthier pulled his gun from his holster. The word Disharmony sparkled along the side of it. Balthier leveled it to the sapere's head as his finger rocked on the trigger. "The difference is, sapere, that if I kill you, the dragons don't give a damn. On the other hand, I am from the purest of dragons and their champion. If I can't get you to respect me, who is to say that this Shil'mak that you've chosen won't do the same?"

"Her mate is a Ch'bauldi."

Balthier lowered Disharmony, but didn't put his gun away. He glanced at Moonhunter, then back to the cowering sapere. "Very well. We shall take her."

The sapere sighed with relief.

Balthier slid Disharmony back into his holster. "Is that why you have also chosen to hear the words of the Shil'mak?"

"It is. I serve her mate directly." The sapere pushed away the cloth of the robe covering his right shoulder and showed Balthier a tattoo there. The marking indicated that he was the direct servant of a lower class Ch'bauldi dragon family.

"Then let us delay no longer, sapere. We have a world about to be destroyed."

At the center of the Council's property, behind a wrought iron fence at least eight feet high, rested an enormous building at least thirty columns wide and twenty-five columns deep with a triangular roof covering it all. The columns on the outer edges of both sides seemed to glow with daylight pouring through the massive structure, but toward the center it grew darker. The columns seemed to disappear in the darkness.

A female sapere in a red sari with embordered golden lotus blossoms stood waiting at the edge of the structure at the base of a short staircase leading up to it.

The male sapere with Balthier and Moonhunter made a gesture to the guards at the large, iron gates. It took four men to push open the gates and allow them access.

The female sapere knelt on the white marble walkway and bowed with her arms stretched out before her until her head touched the ground, waiting until Balthier and Moonhunter stopped before she gracefully rose. "Noble novihomidrak of the Ch'bauldi, you have been given your directions and your objectives, have you not?"

"We have our directions and our objectives," Balthier confirmed.

She extended a hand toward Balthier, which he took. She slid a ring onto his middle finger. Then she reached out to Moonhunter, who also offered his hand while enjoying the jasmine scent floating around her. He wished he could step closer. She slid an identical ring onto his middle finger. Moonhunter felt the band size itself snuggly around his finger. The black stone had tiny white and blue flecks in it which made it look like a star field. The female sapere leaned over and kissed the stone on the ring, then did the same to Balthier's. "I grant you blessings. Stay safe inside the temple and on your journey. Godspeed."

Moonhunter heard Balthier scoff as they turned away and went up the stairs. "You really have no love of the saperes, do you?" Moonhunter asked. He'd always seen the way that Balthier danced on the edge of protocol and disrespect.

"I don't understand their function any longer," Balthier replied in nearly a whisper. "I don't understand why the Council keeps them around."

"What do you mean?"

"When novihomidraks use to go through the Crossing ceremonies, their purpose was necessary. They were a grounding influence to the novihomidrak."

Moonhunter thought about his wing from earlier. "What about for healing a wounded novihomidrak? Only their magic is capable of that."

"That has a purpose, barely. Understand that we have need for it as novies of pure Ch'bauldi dragons and we have the venomcur. Other novihomidraks of lesser dragons don't have to worry about dying from a cut from a novihomidrak weapon. We retain that special right, all to prove our worthiness." Deciding to end his sarcastic tirade,

Balthier turned and pointed back at the sapere now walking down the stairs. "But that little scene there, it's pure superstitious nonsense. We could cut that out. We don't need saperes whose only function is to give us blessings for trips through the Wells. Send that little sweetheart with us through the Wells to help in case we got hurt, then I might be a little more yielding to their continued necessity."

Moonhunter nodded. "But what if a novihomidrak wanted to go through the Crossing ceremonies, on the off chance? Wouldn't it be necessary for someone to know the ceremonies then?"

"Any idiot could mutter words and phrases and the ceremonies are written down for that reason. I mean, even Serchk could do it, for crying out loud."

Balthier's dislike of Moonhunter being a friend with a sapere ran deep. Balthier usually called it a waste of time, but Serchk understood Moonhunter on a level that Balthier didn't.

"Besides," Balthier continued, "No one wants to go through the ceremonies anymore."

"Why don't you? Did you never have the desire to become even better?" Moonhunter asked even while mentally kicking himself for his blatant questions.

"You sure are being nosey today. Read your instructions again and make sure you've got it. It'll be too dark soon and I don't want you getting us lost."

Moonhunter raised the note and read it again. "Enter at column seventeen. Sixteen columns down, two left, four to the left, three to the right."

Balthier started down the walkway outside of the columns, then turned and leaned back some so he could view the columns behind them. "This is seventeen. So we go sixteen, then two left, four left, three right."

"That's it."

"And our entry word?"

Moonhunter checked the sheet again, then flipped it over to look at the blank back. "There isn't one."

"Dragon vision. The saperes have touched that." There was an edge of angry irritation in Balthier's voice, but whether it was at Moonhunter's forgetful moment or at the thought of the saperes, Moonhunter wasn't sure.

"Right," Moonhunter gasped as he blinked and lowered the red lids down over his eyes. On the sheet, the word became visible. "Pracc'chi."

"Let's find the damn door then."

As they started down the columns, Moonhunter saw Balthier put his left hand out to his side slightly so that his fingers brushed against the columns as they walked by. Balthier turned and Moonhunter saw the dragon lids glowing slightly. "It's getting darker. Stay close."

Moonhunter quickened his pace. Even with his dragon vision, the blackness closed in. He could no longer see his feet on the stone, though there were bright white spots of distant stars becoming visible as if he were walking on space. He also put his hand out to count the columns. Balthier vanished completely from sight.

"We're sixteen down," Balthier called out even as Moonhunter's heart quickened.

"When's the dragon supposed to meet us?" Moonhunter asked.

"Hopefully before we fall through the doorway. Damn Shil'mak dragons!"

Moonhunter saw something beneath the stone floor as if something moved through space. Stars disappeared behind blackness. He swore he saw a green eye looking out at him. "Is that the dragon?"

"What?"

"Below us."

"Damn it. Turn. You distracted me. I'm at the third column."

"Can you come back?" Moonhunter asked, reaching out his hand for Balthier. He hadn't thought the man had gotten that far ahead of him.

"I can't. The stream is awfully thick here. I'm caught in a gravitational pull. Is there a clip?"

Moonhunter reached blindly for the column he knew he stood by and felt along the surface for a loop in the stone. "There isn't. I'll set one."

"I'd hate to say to hurry."

Resisting the urging barb, Moonhunter felt out for the Humline and grabbed a mental hold on the energy. He needed a clip, a hammer, and probably about six feet of cabling. "Vochey."

Weight settled into his pack. He stripped it from his back and unzipped it. Inside, he blindly found the hammer and the clip. He looped the backpack over his arm. He could barely see the column and knew his eyes wouldn't adjust further to the dim light. He placed the piercing end of the clip on the column and struck the head with the hammer, driving the point into the stone. Then he held tightly to it and tried to pull it out. For a second, it slid backwards before the barbs caught and set into the stone. Quickly, he pulled the cable from the bag and hooked it onto the clip. "I'm coming," Moonhunter said.

"Don't go past the opposite column."

"I know." Moonhunter slid a foot out across the stone, hoping his foot would hit the base of the column before he'd gone by it. But they'd never been in this dark of a Wells combination before. They might as well actually be floating through space.

How much further?

The floor pushed up against his lead foot as if someone had pressed against it. Moonhunter dropped his gaze and saw the creature moving under the floor again. He wanted to draw back. "Balthier, there is something beneath the floor."

"Moonhunter, look up. Keep your eyes level. Don't look down. We're going to a galaxy colliding with another. It's bound to cause disturbances in the space around it."

Balthier was right. Warping of space and time was inevitable in the destructive chaos of the universe. All things endured the painful spewing of birth into the world only to experience the cycle of seasons and collapse in death.

Moonhunter stepped forward. His toe knocked against the platform of the column. "How far passed are you?"

"My fingers are still touching the stone."

"I'm going to slide the cable along the column. Hopefully you'll feel it." Moonhunter started lifting the extra cabling up as high as he could and reached around the column, trying to keep it stretched out as straight as it could before it bent under its own weight and began lowering it slowly. Slowly. Then he felt a pull in return.

"Got it," Balthier said.

Moonhunter grabbed the cabling with both hands and began to pull. The stream that Balthier was caught in wouldn't release him. "Can you climb up the cabling?"

"Don't you bloody well think I'm trying?"

The floor rocked beneath Moonhunter and he almost let go of the cabling as he stumbled. The stone cracked. "That wasn't my imagination!"

"Calm down, boy!"

A second earthquake rocked through the temple, actually shaking the columns. The cabling slacked in Moonhunter's hands and he fell to the floor. As he rolled onto his stomach to push himself up, he saw the eye pass beneath him again. He jerked, jumping to his feet and stepping backwards into the cabling. He almost flipped backwards over the suddenly taut line. "Shit! It's a monster, Balthier. I saw it. I can't feel it. Shit, shit, shit."

"It's in space."

"It's attacking the freaking tunnels!"

"Moonhunter, remember where you are."

The words as calm as day acted like a slap across his face. He was in the temple and that was a magically simulated labyrinth created by the dragons to allow for the passage of the novihomidrak through the Wells. But in the magic, it made a novihomidrak experience the branches of the Wells. That included gravitational pulls of the galaxies as well a certain feeling of helplessness at the vastness of all of creation. It was designed for the novihomidrak to feel human once more, minuscule compared to the mission at hand. To stand before ten billion stars of which you are nothing more than a speck on a piece of dust had a way of humbling like no other.

Moonhunter felt Balthier move beside him.

"Besides," the old man growled, "it was the Shil'mak dragon trying to get me back on course."

The Shil'mak dragon? Moonhunter let the statement sink in.

Balthier grabbed his sleeve. "Come on. We've still got two more turns to make. And once we're there, I'm going to kill myself a dragon."

10

The light from below them grew intense as they neared the final turn, lighting up their final columns. The pull of two galaxies crashing together with all their matter being pulled to the centers in a massive tug-of-war made Moonhunter stop and stare. A planet in the middle of the cataclysm was being pummeled by debris that had ripped it to its core. On the opposite side of the planet, where it was currently in the dark of night, there were several orangish groupings of light, indicating a civilization. How many people on the planet had already died. Maybe everyone was, their atmosphere demolished as the first chunk of planet dissolved away. A rock got pulled from the orbit of the planet and slammed into the core, letting a geyser of magma erupt several miles into the air before what was left of the gravitation field pulled it back down.

"Come, Moonhunter," Balthier said, touching Moonhunter's shoulder. "Where we're going is not too far behind that planet."

"But all those people... do you think they knew? Do you think they got off their world before it was destroyed?"

Balthier was silent for a moment and Moonhunter wondered if the older man was reaching out for information from the Humline. He knew he could do the same, but he didn't have the courage. "Some questions are best left unanswered."

Moonhunter knew the resolution was there in Balthier's words: the civilization of that planet had known and had been unable to escape their bubble, let alone their doomed galaxy. He followed Balthier, but his mind remained on the dying planet. All the knowledge, all the art, everything created during their planet's history was eradicated as if it had never existed. Everything would be torn back to its base elements and fed back to the hunger of this chaos. What new life would arise? Would it contain the collective knowledge of that planet, or was that forever lost? What was the point of life if in the end, the true conclusion of the universe which birthed it, everything was wiped clear from the slate?

"Why does the Dragon Council try to save at least a few people from some worlds but not others?" Moonhunter asked.

"Vehlka died so that you would live," Balthier said softly. "I'm sure she would have loved discussing all your questions now and guiding you through these deep feelings. But I think that in her sacrifice, she answered everything you would ever need to know about being a fantastic champion for the universe. Even a question with a difficult moral choice like that."

Moonhunter wondered if being here in the labyrinth had deepened Balthier's connection to the Humline. Or maybe it had eased the gruff barrier he normally had up around his emotions.

Or did this have to do with the Crossing ceremony Moonhunter had already initiated? The part that had interested Moonhunter the most about the novihomidraks' ceremonies was the telekinetic abilities that were said to come with it. That and the wings. If he could read the thoughts of other novihomidraks, how much more quickly could he learn? How much more would he know when an attack launched against him? How much closer to the Humline could he come?

"Are you ready?" Balthier asked. "It's time to go black."

As if they hadn't already had a hard enough time. Moonhunter checked to make sure Serenity and Tranquility were secure, then tapped the black stone on the ring. A bubble formed around him and he saw the mostly translucent shell form around Balthier as well.

Moonhunter nodded as Balthier waved his hand over a space in the wall which looked entirely black. "Pracc'chi," Balthier said.

As if an airlock had been opened, the black portal dropped and Moonhunter felt himself sucked into the realm beyond along with Balthier. They fell directly into the Wells. In the next instance, they were grabbed in the large clawed hands of the Shil'mak dragon. Everything around them darkened to black so that Moonhunter could no longer see Balthier in his shell and could only see the pads of the dragon's hand pressing against his own shell. The Shil'mak yawed to the right, then dove fast and hard that the motion sent Moonhunter tumbling in his bubble. He landed on his back. The riser and delicately curved limbs of his bow, Tranquility, pressing into his spine.

The world exploded into light as they emerged out of a Well. The Shil'mak dropped them onto a stone platform. The shell broke off Moonhunter and dissolved. On all fours, he noticed that the platform was surrounded by grass, freshly cut that he could taste the green in his mouth. People were around him. As he got to his feet, the Shil'mak landed nearby. Moonhunter did his best to remain on his feet, but the force of the dragon's wings along with the vertigo of traveling through the dark Wells knocked him back to his knees. He felt Balthier reach down and drag him up.

"Drink the herme's milk off of the pit," a man said before Moonhunter had a chance to finish assessing his surroundings. A cup of white liquid was shoved under him with something that looked like a fuzzy, flat bone sticking out of the cup.

"Do it, Moonhunter," he heard Balthier say.

With shaking hands, Moonhunter reached for the handleless cup and took it from the sapere offering it. His fingers could barely grab onto the furry fruit pit which stuck up from the glass. Somehow, he got it to his mouth and he sucked the white milk off, then dipped it back for more.

"Herme's milk helps with the shakes from Well travel," the sapere said as if they were novihomidraks who had never been through the tunnels before. Of course, Moonhunter was use to walking around with his head in his hands until the shakes went away.

As Moonhunter went to suck the fruity milk off the pit for the fourth time, the sapere pulled the cup from his hands. "Not too much," the sapere warned.

"I'm still shaking," Moonhunter protested as the cup left his fingers. He wished he could focus to make his hands fight for the cup. Instead, Moonhunter turned around.

The Well they had just emerged from sat in the center of a courtyard. Five more males all draped in green and gold, Nefterru saperes, stood around them, no female saperes in the count. Beyond them down in the grass, brilliant red and gold curtains hung between three columns, acting as partial walls to give the platform semi-privacy. Moonhunter noticed the stiffness to the material as it swung lightly in the breeze, and realized there was no way it was cloth. Putting his head in his hands as he knew he would, he staggered to the edge of the platform and lowered his dragon lids for a closer look at the curtain. It was actual dragon scale. Ch'bauldi dragon scales.

"Balthier?" Moonhunter couldn't look away long enough to see if Balthier had noticed him or his motioning arm.

Balthier grabbed his arm and dragged him in the opposite direction toward an opening. "Not now, Moon. We have work to do, remember?"

"Didn't you notice—"

"You should take a rest," one of the saperes said.

"Not now!"

Moonhunter, suspecting that Balthier was actually shouting at him rather than the saperes, took the hint. He followed Balthier from the courtyard through a gated exit, vaguely remembering that Balthier had been here before and knew the way. "Right. What are we here for now?"

"There's a scientist on this planet, one of the most brilliant minds of his time for this world. We need to get him off." Balthier closed his eyes. "Attune yourself to this world's Humline."

Right, Moonhunter thought. They were on a new world with a different energy running through it. Moonhunter closed his eyes and let himself sink into the vibration of this world until he heard it zinging through him, a blue energy line that carried the humming sound of the history and future of this planet.

Balthier looked back in the direction of the temple

courtyard. "We're not being followed. We don't want to walk around on the street with our weapons visible, so we should cloak them." Once their weapons were hidden, Balthier tagged Moonhunter's arm as he began to move forward. "Let's go."

Moonhunter felt his bearings beginning to return as they walked along the concrete sidewalk. Freshly mown lawn covered the ground on both sides with an occasional oak tree casting shady spots for picnics. It felt like they were in a park surrounded by a tall skyscraper city. There was a large fountain in the middle of the area where several people were currently gathered. Several sidewalks criss-crossed the grassy area, all leading to the fountain and out to staircases that left this peaceful little hollow for the city beyond. While everything here seemed green and white, the skyscrapers were all black and metallic silver, sunlight sparking off darkened windows. Moonhunter heard the hum of motors moving in the distance. And the sky was a brilliant purple, marred by a broken line of bright blue and white. "That's the light from the colliding galaxy?"

"Yeah. It's still light years away, but they see it coming."

"How terrifying."

"They've been seeing it for thousands of years, generation after generation. It's normal to them. Look, we're here to get the scientist and his family," Balthier reminded Moonhunter. "Nothing more. We can't save this planet or anyone else on it."

Moonhunter couldn't help but to think of all the literature, art, and knowledge from this world that would be lost in its destruction. The whole sum of what this civilization had become gone in a cosmic blink of the eye.

He glanced toward the fountain again where he saw several little girls dancing around in the spraying water. They might as well be corpses. Would their parents hold them in their arms as their world crumbled or would they choose to end their children's lives before their planet started to come apart?

"Mind your thoughts, Moon," Balthier warned with a tone softer and gentler than normal. "It reads on your face."

Moonhunter tried to shift all the depressing thoughts out of his head, but he couldn't get the ache from his heart. He chose to say nothing as he followed Balthier.

They came out on the street where cars hummed along both rolling on the road and flying above in rows at different levels. Closer to the park, several pieces of sculpture lined the sidewalk. Each piece, a creation of someone's hands. Moonhunter wondered how many centuries this artwork had been around. Were the artists still alive? Did they have museums and galleries where more art was shown? Did they have vast collections of artists from the past? Was an entire history about to be erased from the whole of the universe as if they had never lived? Had there been wars fought here for territory that would no longer exist? Why hadn't they learned to co-exist with one another instead and worked to get off this rock? Why had they stayed trapped in their bubble instead of freeing themselves from a certain death?

"Moon?"

Moonhunter realized he'd stopped to look around and that Balthier had gotten much further ahead.

"Coming," he said as he picked up his pace to catch up with Balthier. "Everyone seems so calm, going about their business. Are there plans to evacuate this planet? They have technology to have flying cars and build skyscrapers. Is no one doing anything to save them from their fate?"

A gray cast came over Balthier's face. His lips set tightly as he looked at the ground as if to watch the mechanical movements of his feet walking beneath him. "It's best if you don't think about it."

Moonhunter realized that was a 'no' answer. "Shouldn't we do something about it? Are we not champions for the inhabitants of the universe? Are they not worthy—"

"Stop!" Balthier growled. "I told you not to think about it."

"But—"

"No! There are somethings we cannot change, no matter how much we wish we could." Balthier kicked at a stone on the path. "As novihomidraks, we have to see that there is a higher purpose even in chaos and destruction."

Moonhunter wished this was one of those moments when he could just take off and fly away. Why had Balthier insisted that he come on this mission with him? He would have been happier staying at the pools, not knowing that this world, so very far away from his own, was about to be turned to dust along with all the inhabitants. Yes, he knew that at the core this was all energy and energy could not be destroyed, only transformed, but that didn't make it any easier. Yes, these people were just shells which housed a slice of the Universal Spirit running through all things. The Humline told him that every time he touched it. But right now they were people with lives that wanted to be lived. They didn't know, not like he did, that other lives were waiting for them. Any sorrow and joy they didn't experience in this life would be enjoyed in another. Their souls longed to create and it was in these shells that the soul fulfilled its every desire. He knew that. But they didn't. They would know fear and pain as their world tore itself to pieces. Yes, on some level, each one had universally asked for this. On their human level, each one would bleed and die. His stomach churned as a vertigo hit him and sent the ground wobbling beneath his feet.

"Moon!" Balthier shouted again as Moonhunter had fallen behind again.

"So we're here for a scientist and his family?"

"Yes."

"You said you messed this mission up once already. What happened?"

"I was told to bring the scientist back at any cost," Balthier said, looking at Moonhunter with a softened glance, as if his eyes alone could tell Moonhunter that he understood the compassion Moonhunter felt for the inhabitants of this planet. "Just him. He refused to leave without his family. I couldn't take them."

"So you just went home?"

"I was told to shoot him and bring him back. I couldn't. I went back to the council and refused to come back until they allowed me to retrieve his family as well."

Moonhunter couldn't stop staring at Balthier. "You must have been young."

"Why do you say that?"

"Because you've never been afraid to shoot anything."

"You're right. I was young. But that's just it. I was afraid that if I shot the scientist, it would kill him. I didn't think I could just stun him."

Moonhunter felt like there was a larger lesson here that Balthier was trying to pass on, but what exactly was it? Sometimes it would be easier if his mentor just spoke exactly what was on his mind.

"And the saperes... they had Ch'bauldi scales hanging like trophies... what was that about? Don't they care they are on a world about to die?"

"They were trophies. The hatred of Nefterru dragons towards the Ch'bauldi runs that deeply, and even the saperes hold that prejudice to heart." Balthier sighed. "Don't worry. They will be evacuated from the planet soon, probably after our mission, which is the only reason a few select volunteers have remained here as it grows more dangerous. We should count ourselves lucky that they didn't poison the herme's milk to purify us. That's probably another reason the Council didn't want us arriving on a young, small Ch'bauldi; it might have ended our lives."

Moonhunter gave a shiver, suddenly understanding a little more why Balthier disliked saperes. Novies had to trust them way too much. While a novi couldn't die from poison, that didn't mean that it wouldn't knock them out for a while. In that time while they were unconscious, a biased sapere could do a lot of damage, especially to the novihomidrak of a Ch'bauldi with the venomcur running in a thin layer just beneath their skin.

A girl roller-skated by them, giving a little wave to Moonhunter as she went. Moon turned, noticing that she did the same. She smiled at him as she rolled backwards away from him. Her ponytail did a little flip as she whirled back around and continued on.

"Youth is wasted on the young," Balthier muttered. "Don't get distracted."

"Sorry. It's just…"

"What?" Balthier snapped. "You need to look at young, pretty girls? You don't have enough of them distracting you back home, like Sundancer? Boys!"

"I just…" he began again, still unsure of what more he wanted to say. What were the words he wanted to follow with? Just what?

"Check in with yourself," Balthier said, obviously noting the same thing that Moon realized.

And Balthier was right. He took a breath, letting

himself be filled with peace and exhaling all the tension of the moment. He knew he had to control it.

Control what?

Control his reaction?

His reaction to what?

To letting everyone die on this planet as it once again returned to stardust. Yes, the girl on the roller-skates was about to become nothing.

Was that the truth he felt?

No, he knew the truth of the Wells. He knew, yes he knew, that death was only an illusion. Every soul was but a touch of the life force from the all. It couldn't really be destroyed. It just moved from one body to another. Even the outward form of the bodies changed. The roller-skating girl would be born again, maybe as a tree, or a dog, or a rock, or even another girl. Heck, with the principle of time, she could be reborn as him. Had she been looking at her future self? Or had he been staring at his future self? Was that why they'd been drawn to look at each other?

So, just what?

"I just felt a connection, that's all," Moonhunter said. "Just a connection." As he said the words, he felt a strong pull to the roller-skating girl. Damn it was strong. He wanted to turn and run after her. "Are you sure we can't save anyone else from this planet?"

"The scientist and his family. That's all," Balthier stated.

Would it be too much to ask for the girl to be in the scientist's family? Could he dare to hope? His gaze drifted toward the large tear in the sky. It hadn't changed, at least not to his perception, but he knew that out there in space, chaos was destroying everything around that ribbon. He felt so insignificant and powerless in the midst of it. He couldn't even help one girl.

"The scientist is probably at his lab," Balthier said. "He's usually there until dark. We should get him first. It'll be easier to explain to his family if he's there to do it."

"Lead on," Moonhunter said, his gaze still looking after the girl, except now he had to use his dragon vision to do so.

"Moon!"

Moonhunter blinked away the extra lids and looked innocently at Balthier. "I'm coming."

"Yeah, well I need your thoughts and body in this too, not just your brain."

"We're here. I mean, I'm here. Let's do this."

11

Balthier and Moonhunter walked a couple blocks away from the park where the skyscrapers glistened in the afternoon sun with shiny silvers and blacks. People on the streets wore dark suits, several pulling on sunglasses as they exited buildings and hurried along the sidewalks. It all had a formal, mechanical feel to it as if these men and women were going about the motions of daily life without heed to the overall picture. No one looked up toward the ribbon stretching ominously across the sky.

Moonhunter swore that the only difference between each of the skyscrapers was the large number on the outside of each building. The problem was that nearly every block had repeating numbers. He figured it had to be some sort of gridding system so that the locals of the planet could find their way around. Right now, they were on Frenlin, which seemed to have no direction, and Hargl North, but across the street was Hargl East.

"Epically confusing," Moonhunter muttered as they waited to cross the intersection.

"Tell me about it," Balthier said. "I didn't know where I was going the last time and it took me three days just to figure out their system."

Once they were across the street, Balthier grabbed Moonhunter's shoulder and pulled him aside. After digging in his pocket, Balthier pulled out a little capsule and handed it to Moonhunter. "Swallow this."

"Nano?" Moonhunter asked, looking at it.

Balthier tossed a capsule of his own into his mouth and swallowed it. "They're programmed to act like the identity chips the citizens of this planet are injected with at birth. Come on, eat up. They'll need a moment to get where they need to."

Moonhunter swallowed the capsule just as Balthier muttered an exclamation of pain and grabbed the back of his neck.

"Did I mention that they have to work their way into your spinal fluid?" Balthier said with a grin.

As they started to cross Hargl East, Moonhunter felt the pinch in the back of his neck and he reached up to feel it.

"Don't rub it," Balthier said, knocking Moonhunter's hand back. "Do you really want squished nanos swimming around under your skin?"

Moonhunter shivered at the idea. Balthier was kidding; nanos flushed out through the bloodstream in time, but still…

They entered one of the tall skyscraper buildings. As soon as they were through the welcoming doors all lit in sunlight, they passed through security gates. Moonhunter heard the buzzing of their wireless transmittal signal, something unperceived by most beings, and the harsh sound made his head spin. "Tell me you heard that one," Moonhunter said. "That was as loud as a freight train."

"Nope, didn't hear it," Balthier said, "and you have no idea how loud a freight train is."

"I've seen the microvids."

"Microvids!" Balthier stalked across the tiled entryway toward the elevators.

The shaded lobby windows didn't allow in any of the beautiful light from outside. High above them were several artificial lights set into the ceiling. It made the building feel sterile and cold. Maybe scientists didn't like nature. It filled Moonhunter with chills.

The elevator also held a barren feeling as they stepped in and were surrounded by stainless steel. Only the keypad was black. The buttons showed signs of depression from being pushed so many times, but otherwise it was flat and textureless. Balthier pressed the five button and the elevator started to glide upwards.

"Reminds you of being in the pearl, doesn't it?" Balthier said with a longing sigh.

"No, it doesn't." Moonhunter said, not giving into Balthier's drollness.

"Show some humor, boy."

"I'm not in the mood for your glib wit. We're saving one person from a planet about to be destroyed. I find that a little depressing."

"Fine, wallow."

Moonhunter had expected another stern warning from Balthier about staying in the game, and was surprised when it didn't come.

The elevator stopped and the door dinged as the door opened.

Balthier stepped out and looked around. "Um…"

"Yes?"

"We're on the fifth floor, right?"

Moonhunter pointed at the little plaque by the elevator door. "Five."

Balthier turned in a circle. Moonhunter looked down the hallways, which had several doors going off in each direction. It looked like a typical office building. What could Balthier be seeing that he wasn't?

"These walls," Balthier said, "not here before. Level five opened right up into the lab."

"Wrong building?" Moonhunter asked, even as he knew that it was the correct building Balthier had been in before. "Remodel?"

Balthier saw a building map on the wall nearby and moved over to it. After a moment of looking it over, letting his finger lead the way over the map, he closed his eyes and Moonhunter felt his essence reach out. After a moment, he opened his eyes and responded, "He's not here. The government has moved him. We'll have to get him at his home."

"The government came in and had this guy's lab moved and the entire floor remodeled? Who is this scientist?"

"He's a mechanical scientist."

"Mechanical scientist?" Moonhunter asked as he got back in the elevator behind Balthier. "There are thousands of mechanical scientists throughout the galaxy."

Balthier hit the button to return them to the ground level. "How many of them work with dark matter?"

"Dark matter? He's a dark matter mechanical scientist? Is that even possible?"

"Now you know why he's got to be saved. We'll go back down stairs and check for his name on the directory just in case. We're looking for Dr. Melstone. If we don't find him here, we'll go to his home. Last I knew, he was living in Tarvey on Andrew Street."

Moonhunter hung onto all the information, knowing it might be important for him to remember on his own at some point.

The elevator slowed to a stop, shuddered, and then the door slid open on the ground floor. Several armed guards stood waiting, rifles and pistols raised. "Hands up," the man in the center shouted. His black, straightline jacket had golden buttons on white trim, making him look more official than several of the other men in plain black shirts and caps.

Moonhunter caught Balthier's sidelong glance as Balthier slowly started to put his hands in the air.

"Let's talk about this," Balthier said, "before one of your men gets hurt."

One of the men, whose black uniform also had white trim though no decoration, snickered and received a glare from his commander.

"I'm looking for someone and got a little lost. I think I'm in the wrong building," Balthier said. "I don't want any trouble."

The commander firmed his grip on the pistol he held pointed toward Balthier. "We know who you are. Balthier Foulbreath, you are wanted for the destruction of the wave tower and the deaths of five military men and two civilians. Come peacefully or we will take you by force. Turn around."

Balthier began to slowly turn, Moonhunter following his lead. "Foulbreath?" Moonhunter mouthed. Balthier shrugged with a passing grin.

"Lieutenant, check them for weapons."

The man who had snickered moved in, cautiously putting his weapon away, then heading toward Moonhunter who was closer to him. Moonhunter waited impatiently for Balthier to indicate what they were going to do.

They might not find the bow hidden on Moonhunter's back, but the dagger hanging from his side would be an issue when the man patted down Moonhunter's sides and the lieutenant's hands hit something unseen. The lieutenant's shaking fingers drew closer.

"Are you really going to let them arrest us?" Moonhunter asked in the dragon tongue.

"The boy has nothing to do with this. He's an ignorant foreigner who was in the elevator with me," Balthier said over his shoulder. "Let him go and I'll go peacefully with you."

"Balthier?" Moonhunter whispered.

"He has been seen on surveillance with you entering the building. He is an accessory to whatever terrorism you have planned now. He will also be detained." The commander moved forward to handcuff them.

Balthier turned back around, shoved the lieutenant to the floor, and stepped up to the commander. The commander's gun fired right into Balthier's stomach, making him double over from the force of the impact. The bullet hit the ground. Grunting, Balthier stood up, one arm over his middle. "Now see, I can't let you do that. We're both on a mission and unfortunately I stand higher than your law. I tried to play along and give you a chance to resolve this, but I can't let you take both of us in."

Balthier pushed the commander backwards, knocking him to the ground. One of the other guards took a shot at Balthier. It knocked him forward, but the bullet deflected and sank into the metal of a nearby wall.

"This is why innocent people got hurt last time," Balthier said, straightening. "You cannot hurt us."

The guard was shaking now. "Are you angels or demons?"

"Neither. We're dragon born." Balthier stepped around

him. "Please don't fire upon us again. Your weapons cannot hurt us."

Moonhunter started to walk away, Balthier coming up right next to him.

"Halt!" the man shouted after them. "Halt or we will fire."

They were halfway across the lobby when the shots began. Moonhunter felt the first one slam into his shoulder. The force knocked him forward in a sideways angle. His hip took the second hit. He stumbled, but before he hit the floor, Balthier towed him back to his feet.

One of the huge lobby windows shattered, raining glass down on them. Sunlight flooded the building. Holding onto each other's arm, Balthier and Moonhunter ran. Outside, sirens wailed in the distance. An alarm was sounding from the building they had just left and people in the vicinity were scattering. Many ran in a crouched position not realizing that it slowed their movements and increased their chances of becoming a victim more than if they had dashed for cover.

Moonhunter and Balthier ran across the street, fleeing toward the park as the first patrol car arrived on the scene.

"They've alerted the scientist to our presence and are moving him," Balthier said. Moonhunter knew that 'they' meant the authorities of this world.

"Already?" Moonhunter asked as he glanced back over his shoulder. "How could they know our purpose here? We only just arrived."

"Don't you think I know that?"

Moonhunter threw his hand in the air. "That's not an answer to my question."

"I know that too." Balthier quickened his pace, but looked back over his shoulder to Moonhunter. "The scientist obviously told them about my last visit and they suspected I might be back to try to kidnap him again. I'm sure my face is on their recognition program and the second we stepped into that elevator we were flagged. They probably went to rescue him immediately."

"So if they're already ahead of us, how do we get ahead of them?"

"I get captured and you get out of here."

"I hate that plan."

"I know you do. Do it anyway."

Balthier stopped suddenly and turned. Moonhunter saw the punch coming, but he was already stepping into Balthier's swing. His dragon shielding went off before he could decide if he wanted to take the blow or not, like he'd even had a choice. The shielding knocked Balthier backwards and sent him ungraciously somersaulting over the pavement.

Kneeling down, Moonhunter found Balthier unconscious. He heard shouts behind him and knew that authorities were already dashing for them. Take the assailants while they were down. Did he dare try to heft Balthier over his shoulder and run? That wasn't what his mentor had wanted him to do. Moonhunter knew he couldn't let the confused thoughts of those around him cloud his own judgement, nor could he stop. He had to move and fast. Leaving Balthier, Moonhunter started running.

12

Some of the footfalls behind Moonhunter silenced as people stooped to handcuff Balthier, but part of the divided group continued on after Moonhunter. Worse, they were gaining on him. There were no alleyways for him to duck down, no shadows to hide in. Everywhere was brightly lit beneath this planet's sun. He sensed that they expected him to run to the park fountain and hide among the people there, so Moonhunter went in the opposite direction. How exactly did the Onesong want him to get out of this predicament? He didn't even have a moment to feel along the Humline for an answer. He just had to keep moving.

He chanced a glance back and saw Balthier being shoved into a squad car. How would he find Balthier if he couldn't follow where they were taking him?

Yet he could and he knew it. He continued running for the park, nearly running over the girl on the skates as her path nearly collided with his. "Sorry!" he yelled. He hit the grass and rolled. The air felt so much cooler than it had when he'd been on the sidewalk.

"Hey!" the girl screamed as his pursuing party also rushed by her. "People are skating here!"

The entire park seemed flat, interspersed with oak trees providing both sun and shadow to the area. The trees, each perfectly manicured into umbrella tops as if they were right from a child's drawing, provided good shade along the grass, but no cover for Moonhunter to hide or low branches for him to climb.

Flashing yellow and red lights appeared on the other side of the park. Reinforcements had been called in.

If only he could fly. Then he could soar off above the oaks and leave everyone behind. He might even be able to follow Balthier and free him.

Moonhunter searched for a good break in the trees while nerves filled him. He had one chance at this, knowing very well that his capture was assured if he fell flat on his face.

His wings were too small and brittle. If he popped it out, or worse broke a bone, he'd not likely get help from the Nefterru saperes once they saw the Ch'bauldi coloring.

But if he got heat beneath him, like he did in the cabin while he and Balthier were in space, he might get enough lift. Once he had a cushion of air beneath him, he only had to maintain it. With ground effect, he wouldn't even have to be high in the air. He could fly low, where he wouldn't be hurt badly if he fell. He could zip away, leaving the chase behind him.

He wouldn't know if he didn't try.

He filled his lungs with as much air as he could while running. Then he thought about his wings extending. They broke free from beneath his skin and tore his shirt. He tried to free himself from the tattered remains of the cloth. Exhaling and making the air in front of him as hot as he could, he opened his wings full to the sides and leaned forward. Within a couple steps, he felt his toes leave the ground. As much as he wanted to shout in triumph, he didn't; he wasn't clear yet.

But he was floating. His wings gave an experimental beat. His body rose.

When he tried again and found himself lift higher, he realized he was flying on his own.

Tree branches snatched at his wings. They knocked him off balance and he careened dangerously to the side. A larger branch caught him and he smacked onto the trunk, hugging onto it to keep from falling.

Moonhunter searched for an exit, finding only a small one near the top. He'd have to gain momentum, from now being at a complete stop, increase altitude and speed, then tuck his wings in while having enough motion to not then fall from the sky. He was much too much of a novice to pull this off. He might be better off to drop back down to the ground and surrender, though that wouldn't make Balthier very happy.

The fastest of the people chasing him were now beginning to gather at the base of the tree. Moonhunter couldn't hear what was being said, but weapons were being raised toward him and that was all the communication he needed. With another deep breath and a push away from the tree, he exhaled and flapped. A draft caught under his wings and lifted him, then he was soaring upwards.

He approached the gap in the branches. Sky and freedom lay beyond. He held a glide longer than he wished, even felt himself dropping just a little, then he thrust and tucked his wings in against his body. He closed his eyes.

Sunlight shone on his face and his eyelids suddenly seemed yellow. He was through.

Breaking above the trees, he opened his wings once

more and turned toward where he'd last seen the squad car Balthier was being put in. Maybe he could follow from the air. Would the police officers see him pursuing them?

"Damn!" he heard a voice bellow from beneath him. "Get a heli in the air to track him. Quick before he lands somewhere."

Moonhunter pressed on, using heated breath to help support himself. He felt more like a hot air balloon than a hang-glider, but at least his wings were working. He couldn't wait to tell Serchk.

Already the shouting faded behind Moonhunter and the silence of the air took over. As he looked down at the people below him, realizing how small they all were yet being able to recognize the skating girl by the sun reflecting off her black helmet. The girl looked up at him, shielded her eyes from the sun, and waved.

At least someone besides himself was amused at his flight. He wished he dared to impress her with a dip and a flip, but he didn't have enough confidence yet. Besides, now was not the time for showing off. He had to rescue Balthier.

He soared over the tops of the high rises and a thrill went through him a second time: he was flying. On his own. Without having to be in space.

Now that he could see the expanse of the city from above, he realized that squares like the park he had flown out of were scattered throughout a large urban area of concrete and skyscrapers. Beyond the commercial park where they had entered, roads were strung between sections as if most of them had been torn away to make room for more buildings. In some areas there were no cars at all. A few vehicles flew in the air above the roads too, moving faster than the traffic on the roads.

Parking garages along the edges of various sections had

posted large signs which read: RENT HERE! At the bottom, it read: Airsters always available. Were the flying vehicles called Airsters here?

Moonhunter saw various names listed below the words. Rarely did any of the names repeat. Once again, he had the feeling that the people of this world either had to really know their way around or had to be very smart.

He tilted in the air, yawing as he glided around the building to follow the squad car into an area which had no other cars. They turned on their sirens and pedestrians began to move to the side to allow the car right of way along the sidewalks. Soon, it disappeared into a building.

Moonhunter searched for a place to land. He'd prefer something up a level or two where he could have the high ground and work his way down to Balthier, but there were no balconies or platforms to this building. His only landing spots were near the entry to the underground garage where the car had gone, or by the front door, which had armed sentry standing watch. He doubted they were prepared to take on a novihomidrak, but why take the chance?

On the other hand, Balthier had been insistent on Moonhunter going to get the scientist. Now that Moonhunter knew where Balthier would be held in custody, he knew he ought to go get the scientist. Continue the mission; that's what Balthier would say to him. What were they going to do? Hurt a novihomidrak?

Moonhunter pressed higher into the sky. His hips were beginning to hurt; he hadn't expected that to be a side-effect of flying, but at least now he knew that he'd need to work on strengthening his lower abdomen and hips.

A noise whizzed by him and a metal shell-like body slammed into his. Knocked off guard, Moonhunter tumbled through the air. He felt himself losing altitude.

The black oval rushed him again. Moonhunter

grabbed onto it, his fingers taking a tight hold on the ridges of its metallic body. The drone buzzed and tried to break free. Moonhunter held on even as it began to drag him. He no longer had to put much effort into maintaining flight, though he didn't have much control over the direction.

"Take me to your leader," Moonhunter laughed.

The engines cut out and the drone turned to dead weight in his arms. They plunged.

Moonhunter let himself fall, dropping the drone at the last possible chance, before extending his wings to stop his rapid descent. His body jerked as it caught in the updraft, then he settled onto the ground. Not bad for his first landing. He'd always thought that would be the hardest part.

As he went to check out the drone, it zipped straight up into the air and stopped at Moonhunter's eye level.

"Surrender," a voice shouted through some tinny speakers at Moonhunter. "You are under arrest by the Sakaret Police Department. Put your hands behind your head and get down on your knees. Any attempt to resist will result in electroshock."

"Really?" Moonhunter asked. "You expect me to wait around to be arrested?"

"Hands behind you head, down on your knees. This is your final warning."

Moonhunter turned to walk off.

Blue electricity crackled in the air and struck Moonhunter. He felt his hair rise up. As the intensely hot shock went through his body, his dragon aspects flared to life. His teeth descended as he turned toward the drone. Talons came out to shred it. Much to Moonhunter's surprise, the drone didn't stop as he took a firm grip of it. His talons wouldn't pierce its metal body, but rather deflected off its ridges.

The power level intensified, which only made Moonhunter's anger grow proportionally. It thrust a net out around Moonhunter, insuring that he couldn't toss the drone away from him. He felt his head spinning and knew that he was about to pass out. No amount of voltage that it could put into him would kill him, but that didn't mean that it didn't hurt and that it wouldn't surpass his pain threshold, which was quickly being reached.

Though he couldn't cut through the metal body, his talons did shred the netting around him. The drone spit a second mesh out as well as once again upping the voltage in its shock weapon.

Moonhunter growled, low and deep, and it nearly scared him. He'd never had that much anger come through him. The rumble gave way to a scream of pain and rage. From his throat and back by his jaws, he felt something spew from his mouth over the drone. Then the metal was melting in his hands. So red and hot the drone's surface had become that he was forced to drop it. It fell to the ground, rolling limply at his feet as it made an awkward sound, snapped once, and relented.

Moonhunter took a jumping step back away from it. "Wow!" He looked down at his reddened hands, knowing they wouldn't be that way nor would they continue to feel raw for very long, but he wanted to know if he'd caused any damage to himself. He couldn't really tell. Balancing himself, he tentatively reached out and kicked the oozing mass with his boot. It rolled in a pool of goo, but seemed dead enough that made him confident enough to kneel down for a closer inspection. He knew he probably shouldn't be lingering here, but this, whatever he had done, was new to him. He wanted a moment to try to figure it out. He'd felt something emerge from his throat. Fire, acid, electricity, he didn't know what the base of it was, but it had been powerful enough to decimate the drone and its abilities nearly immediately. Was this his dragon breath?

He needed to move on. More of those drones might be tracking him down right now.

Already, the ooze was beginning to solidify. Moonhunter could hear Balthier lecturing him about leaving behind evidence that a mundane could investigate. What he wouldn't give for the older man's advice now. He had to hurry and make a decision.

He coughed, trying to hack up some more of whatever he'd just ejected from himself, but nothing came from his pathetic attempts, which even he found laughable. If he felt that he couldn't tell Balthier about his wings, what made him think he could ever explain what had just happened to Balthier.

Energy shifted and Moonhunter heard voices as well as excited barks. They were tracking him with dogs now. He could hear the hounds' claws scratching on the cement.

Drawing to his feet, Moonhunter swept his dragon vision gaze around the surrounding area. A man in a business suit was just getting off a moped a short distance away. Moonhunter began to run as the man took off his helmet.

Moonhunter didn't stop running until he reached the man and knocked him over. "Sorry!" Moonhunter shouted as he took the keys to the moped. "You'll get it back. Let's just hope it's in one piece."

"Hey! Wait!" the man screamed.

Moonhunter started the moped, spun it around, and charged off down the street as the man tried to give chase but fell behind quickly. Moonhunter rode it to the nearest parking garage, knowing that he needed to change vehicles. The moped didn't have any speed or power behind it, nor was it capable of flight, something he sorely needed right now. At least flight without his own wings carrying him. In an Airster, he'd blend in a little better. Disappearing among the masses was something he needed to do right now. Blending in with other humans was the greatest defensive power a novihomidrak had.

The first garage didn't advertise Airsters, so he continued on to the second. Traffic grew thick and he began weaving in and out between cars, ignoring the honks and insults thrown at him as he went. As one driver hollered a particularly nasty expletive at him, Moonhunter wanted to strike out in anger. Then he realized the man would soon be dead. Everyone on this planet was doomed. It made him pause with a moment of sadness.

He wanted to save these people. He couldn't. Balthier had made that quite plain.

What good was being a novihomidrak if he couldn't save the worlds he wished to? Okay, so it was mostly a world of high rises and concrete, but they had tried to restore some of nature's balance to it. They were trying.

A car swerved in front of him, making Moonhunter turn the moped and nearly tip it over on its side. He felt the machine start to go into a slid and threw his weight in the other direction to upright himself again. He raced by the car and waved at the driver as he sped into the parking garage. Moonhunter tucked between the wall and the gate rail, then took the ramps heading toward the upper floors. He was operating on the assumption that Airsters would take off from the upper levels, leaving the lower ones for the cars. The moped's tires felt slick against the cement, making harsh squeaking noises as the tread tried to get a grip. The squealing worsened when he went around corners and up the ramps. For a moment, he had to ask himself if running would be faster. Maybe taking the stairs was an even better option.

Ditching the moped by a stairwell, he ran up several floors. When the police officers discovered the abandoned vehicle, they wouldn't be certain if he'd taken a car or an Airster, not until they researched further to see what had been stolen. Moonhunter hoped that would give him at least a few moments more.

The metal door labeled "Airster Rental Here" greeted him and as he yanked it open, he briefly wondered what was required to legally rent an Airster. It would throw the police off his track for even longer if they had to start flashing his picture around hoping to spark some worker's memory or dig through records for a receipt.

The sound of sirens came through the open gaps in the walls. Moonhunter listened and realized they were surrounding the building. He didn't have long.

Rushing to the first craft, he found that they were magnetically locked down. He looked around for a way to rent and found a board not too far away. Rushing over to it, he read the instructions. Select Airster, insert license, pay, wait for chime, then Airster will unlock.

Moonhunter needed a different plan. He had neither a license issued by this planet nor the local currency.

A man walked through the door behind him. Moonhunter walked away from the board as if he were leaving, but rather moved off slowly to wait by the door. He lowered his dragon lids and looked through the red veil dropped over the grayness of the garage toward the board where the man was currently selecting the Airster in slot R2.

Moonhunter swept his gaze around and saw the machine in that location. It made him grin. Of all the Airsters here, that one probably had the sleekest body of them all. Now whether that was one that the man usually selected or if it just happened to be one that would take him away from the door that Moonhunter still stood by – beware of lurkers – Moonhunter wasn't certain. Regardless, as the man started walking toward it, Moonhunter began to run.

"Sorry. Wish I didn't have to do this," Moonhunter shouted. "Great taste in design though. Thanks for getting one of the sleek ones."

Moonhunter jumped inside the Airster's open cockpit and felt it dip under his weight. He put his hands on the wheel and pressed the trigger throttle with his index fingers. The Airster didn't move.

"Won't work without this," the man, who had never increased the speed of his stride, said as he held up a green and white card with a magnetic strip on the back of it. "Come on, kid. Time to get out."

"I don't suppose you just want to give me the card," Moonhunter pleaded.

The man shook his head. "I don't. I've had a long day and I just want to get home."

"Even if I told you I've also had a long day and mine has just gotten started."

"Look, kid, just get out. You don't have a weapon and I doubt you've had as much martial arts training as I have. I'm impressed that you knew which Airster I chose from that distance, but you're not taking off with it. Better luck with your next victim."

Moonhunter started to climb out of the Airster and jumped down to the cement floor. His dragon teeth extended. As he straightened, he showed the man his red dragon eyes as he snarled, "You're probably wrong on both counts." He unsheathed his dagger and uncloaked his bow. "I have weapons, and what I am goes beyond martial arts. Now, let's work out a deal, shall we?"

"Take the card." The man threw it at Moonhunter. "I'll rent another."

Moonhunter dismissed Tranquility behind the magical cloak, but kept Serenity at hand and pointed the blade at the man. "On second thought, I said, let's work out a deal, something that will benefit us both." He then slid the dagger into his belt. "I have temporary need of your Airster. I also need directions. Help me get where I need to go, then you may have your Airster back."

The man scoffed. "It's obvious that the one the police are after is you. They should be reaching this floor any moment now. Even if I did agree to go with you, who's to say that the moment you get where you're going, I don't call them and tell them exactly where you are?"

"Go right ahead."

"That means you don't plan on being there long."

Moonhunter reached down for the card. The man came forward and stepped his foot down on it. Moonhunter retracted his fingers before they were smashed and stood up to glare at the man, who smiled at him.

"Fine," the man said, "take me on your little adventure." He lifted his foot from the card and started walking around to the passenger side of the Airster. Opening the door, he climbed in, while Moonhunter retrieved the card and jumped back in.

"That slot there," the man directed, pointing to a slot in the dash. "Have you ever driven one of these before?"

"Not an Airster, but I'm a fairly decent pilot. How hard could it be?"

"Famous last words," the man chuckled.

Moonhunter pressed the card into the slot and felt the engine engage. He set his hands on the wheel once more.

"Pull it to back it up, gently now, brake is on the floor. Yeah, you got the throttle. Good, good."

It wasn't too different than other crafts Moonhunter had piloted, but it helped to have someone guiding him rather than just pushing things at random to see what functioned.

"Okay, your lift point is over there," he said, pointing off toward the right.

Moonhunter saw a short platform which extended from the building. "Speed? Flaps? Anything special to take off?" he asked with a quick glance to the man sitting at his side.

"They rent these things to just about anyone. Don't worry about it."

13

As they neared the lift point, a red light began circling from a beacon overhead and a blue light lit up on the floor. "Craft preparing for departure," a voice boomed.

Moonhunter suddenly realized he had no control over the craft. It was moving on its own.

"Release the wheel," the man said as he reached back for his safety strap. A lid slid out from behind them and went over their heads.

Moonhunter scrambled for his strap as the Airster aligned itself with the lift point and began to roll backwards. He suddenly found, as he looked down to do the buckle, that the seat had puffed out a pillow around his head. He couldn't find the insert for the strap.

The man reached over and grabbed it from him, clicking the pieces together. "You've never even been in an Airster before, have you?"

After being laughed at for years by Balthier, Moonhunter knew the man was mocking him. "I just hate seat belts."

"Well, these vehicles won't go until the safeties are locked and secure. Take your foot off the brake, would you?"

Moonhunter already didn't like the craft moving on its own and not responding to him in any way. The lack of control sent nervous skitters up his spine. As soon as Moonhunter released the pedal, the Airster propelled forward and shot from the building. Moonhunter grasped the wheel once more, steering and trying to find his way out into the stream of Airster traffic. The pillow around his head deflated.

"Now, where were you headed?"

"I'm looking for Dr. Melstone. I believe he lives in Tarvey on Andrew Street."

"Tarvey," the man repeated. "Turn left."

Moonhunter aimed the Airster in the direction and flowed over the road traffic.

"So where are you from?" the man asked with a cautious look to Moonhunter.

"What makes you think I'm from somewhere else?"

"Because you've never been in an Airster, yet you fly it pretty well. You've observed enough to know how things work on the planet and you're being very cautious to not get caught. You're shrewd and not afraid to push the bounds though. You are a man on a mission."

"Very perceptive," Moonhunter said, wishing he could just magic the man to sleep. He wondered if any of the dragon enchantments would work here. Maybe he could just hypnotize the man into sleeping. Yet there was a part of him that was curious as well. "Why did you want to go along?"

The man sat back and chuckled. "I don't get to have adventures anymore. My life has become pretty standard. Same thing day in and day out. Sometimes I just want to get away, you know. I just want to fly away. This might be my only opportunity."

While he hadn't said that his world was doomed, Moonhunter wondered if this man was one of the few that knew the galaxy that held his world was busy crashing into another. Any day now, the effects of the collision would be felt here. Once it started, mass hysteria would take over. There would be looting and killing as people tried to have it all as if any of it would help as the end came. No one could escape the death that would press and disintegrate everyone and everything on this world. Moonhunter had to push it away from his mind.

"What's wrong?" the man asked.

Moonhunter wanted to shout that the world was ending and he didn't want everyone to die. But this wasn't like most worlds that he went to, like a normal mission where there was an evil he could defeat. No, this world's calamity was just the normal workings of the Onesong. "We live in a dangerous universe that is constantly growing and changing," Moonhunter found himself replying. "Life should never be mundane when any day it could be wiped out by something so much larger than ourselves."

"Exactly!" the man said ecstatically.

While Moonhunter longed to tell the man how sorry he was, he pressed a smile to his lips and said, "Enjoy." There wasn't really anything either one of them could do about the world's death sentence, but Moonhunter knew that the memory of the man sitting beside him would now live on in his own memory. As small as that seemed, it was all he could offer. "I look forward to discovering the world through your eyes."

This seemed to please the man.

"So, do I have to stay on the road?" Moonhunter asked, figuring that was a good first question since he really wanted to get the scientist before someone alerted him to Balthier's capture.

"It's preferred, the officers will pay more attention to you if you aren't over the roadways, following orders, but it's really much faster if you cut across country."

"Which way?"

"Go right, about a two o'clock direction."

As much as Moonhunter wanted to tease the man and remind him that he was from off-world, Moonhunter had also had enough dealings with worlds with clocks to know exactly what the man referred to. "Sixty degrees clockwise, check," he said instead.

"Um, maybe more that way," the man corrected.

"Forty degrees clockwise," Moonhunter adjusted, with his voice holding a bit of irritation, but he smiled to let the man know he was just joking. "My name is Moon. What can I call you?"

"Moon? You had those kind of parents, huh?"

Moonhunter shrugged. "Better than Ralph."

"Ralph. That's my name. How did you guess?" the man laughed.

Moonhunter felt his eyes widen. "You're kidding me, right?"

"No. It is Ralph, but I'm actually the fourth one in our family."

Wow, Moonhunter mouthed after turning his head slightly away. That was the Onesong in action.

Another Airster whipped out behind them. Ralph noticed it first and glanced back. "You've picked up an officer. Just relax and keep it steady. Don't go over forty."

Moonhunter looked down at the gauge he really hoped was the speedometer. It currently sat at about thirty-eight. He scoffed, wishing it had a digital read out. This was like so analog. "I thought this was a top of the line vehicle."

Ralph looked at him, then caught a clue as to what he was referring to and chuckled. "Takes more skill to read that. Any idiot can fly something that's mostly automated."

"Another reason you were going for this Airster?" Moonhunter asked. "You were hoping I wanted something more automatic?"

"Hey, don't hold that against me. That was before I realized we'd have a lot of fun together." Ralph raised his hand into the air and waved back at the officer following them.

Moonhunter worried for an instant that Ralph signaled for help, but then the officer slowly fell back and turned off.

"They're looking for one young man," Ralph reminded him. "Knowing you have a passenger, especially one not flailing for assistance, assures them that you're not the one they are looking for." Ralph sat back in his seat, nestling back into the tight-fitting padding. "So, what did you do to get the officers all riled up to want to capture you?"

"I arrived," Moonhunter clipped.

"That bad, huh? Wow. I didn't know the officers also watched out for aliens."

"So you don't have off-world travel? No one's ever left the planet?"

"Oh, we've taken a couple steps off this rock, but we can't even figure out for certain how many planets we have in our solar system. Small planets get downgraded to moons or mini planets, and gas giants declared megaliths. Once, they even talked about debunking all the other planets except for Vergnamet 5 because it was the only other one to have life. After all, a planet has to have life to be anything more than a rock, right?"

"Sure, I suppose." Moonhunter tightened his grip on the wheel. If this planet only had the technology to have hoover cars, but hadn't actually achieved space travel, why was this scientist they were to gather so noteworthy? A dark matter engineer, Balthier had said. But this world had yet to develop full utilization of light matter, so how could Dr. Melstone be so advanced in his experiments, enough to be someone that the Dragon Council wanted to save?

"You know," Ralph began, "you appear to have only two facials expressions: curiosity and puzzlement. The curiosity is more child-like while the puzzlement carries the weight of the world with it. What puts you in such a position to have such a wide dynamic?"

"Are you a shrink or something?" Moonhunter asked.

Ralph laughed and rolled his shoulders back into the seats some more. "Lawyer, with a minor in psychology. I wanted to know when people were lying to me."

"So how am I doing so far?"

"You are very clever, shrewd as I said before, and while you haven't lied to me, you do cloak things in half-truths. But, since you're not on my witness stand, I don't have a need to dig any deeper."

Moonhunter smiled. "It keeps you from being too much of an accomplice on this adventure. Too bad you won't be able to defend me if I get caught."

"Somehow, I don't think you're worried about that. You're worried about other things, yes, but capture isn't one of them." Ralph looked around. "See those trees over there, just beyond that is Tarvey. You might want to swing around to the left and put us back on the road before we get there. Chances are there's an officer waiting there to catch commuters in too much of a hurry to get home that cut over the forest."

Moonhunter followed the instructions and, finding an opening in the elevated traffic, took a slot in the line. Ground traffic had come nearly to a standstill. As they got closer, the discovered the Airsters were being stopped as well. Air patrols were going up and down the line, so Moonhunter didn't dare pull out now. Of course, in staying here he risked being recognized if his photo from one of the building's cameras had gotten a good shot of him earlier.

"Relax," Ralph said. "You have no idea that this has anything to do with you."

"What else could it be?" Had Ralph dealt with enough criminal activity that he could now give Moonhunter an example that would put his mind at ease?

"Could be something as simple as a parade route and they are just trying to keep Airsters from jumping the barriers. A couple cities do this sort of thing for prisoner transfer. Could also be a really bad accident."

Prisoner transfer. "Transfer of a diplomat?" Moonhunter asked, his heartbeat quickening.

"I suppose that's a possibility."

As Moonhunter went to pull out of the line, heedless of the attention that it drew, he saw an escorted caravan coming straight toward him. Had he been alone, he would have just pulled out sharply in front of the vehicles, but he had a passenger to consider. "Hold on," he said, shifting the Airster into reverse. He kept his foot on the brake, waiting, and then, when the caravan was about to pass by them, he released the clutch and the brake and stomped on the gas. The Airster shot backwards, leaving Moonhunter with the impression that this craft had enough propulsion that it could probably leave the planet's orbit. The power left him stunned, until the crash.

His side of the Airster took the hit. They rocked back and forth. For a moment, Moonhunter thought the engine had cut out. He instinctively coaxed the gas and the engine maintained.

Lights flipped on and sirens began to blare around them.

"Hold your position," a voice came over a loud speaker. "Put your hands in the air. Wait for the Striker Officer."

"Sorry, officer," Moonhunter shouted back as he raised his hands up by his head. He wondered how long it would take for this Striker Officer, whatever that was, to approach. Sirens wailed as something moved from behind the lead vehicle. A man heavily coated in body armor came riding forward on a machine that looked like sleek rocket. He stopped and hovered next to the Airster while Moonhunter stared at the Striker's craft in jealousy. Why couldn't he have found something like that? "I'm new to driving an Airster. I didn't realize that I'd put it in reverse. I thought it was neutral."

"Neutral?" the Striker Officer shouted back at him.

"I'm new at it, sir," he repeated, this time, his voice taking on an undertone holding a smooth rumble. "I think you want to take pity on me by telling me who you are escorting out of the area."

"Son, you're new at this," the Striker began. "I think you better land this craft and let your father take over."

"F-father!" Ralph choked.

"Yes, sir," Moonhunter replied. "I'll land right now. Sorry, I just got caught up in the excitement of everything that was going on."

The Striker whipped around and headed back to his position in escort while Moonhunter once again felt jealous over the vehicle's maneuverability. Slowly, Moonhunter began to lower the Airster and watched overhead as the escort line began to move over their heads.

"Did he really call me your father?" Ralph asked. "Do

I look old enough to be your father? Older brother maybe."

While Ralph had his identity meltdown, Moonhunter worried about why his mesmerize hadn't fully succeeded. It had partially; the Striker had accepted the first part of the suggestion, but it had gotten scrambled. One thing he was certain of though was that the person they escorted out was a father and they probably were taking the man's family out as well. Moonhunter counted the vehicles: four large Airsters with six Striker units.

Before Moonhunter actually descended down onto the land traffic, he whipped around and began to follow behind the escort, trying to stay low and far enough back to not be seen by any of the officers above. He blinked down his dragon lids so he could watch for any subtle movements that one of the Strikers saw him trailing behind them.

"Someone's going to notice you, or one of the land bounds are going to call you in for flying too low," Ralph warned.

"Let them. We'll be long gone by the time an officer shows up to check it out."

They continued to fly, staying low and behind the caravan. As far as Moonhunter could tell, no one seemed to notice them. Not a very secure caravan, he thought.

Shouts of alarm went up and for a moment, Moonhunter thought they had been spotted. But through his dragon lids, Moonhunter saw several people of the caravan above pointing toward the sky. Parts of the caravan broke off while others sped up faster. It seemed as if chaos had taken over.

"Blasters! We need blasters upfront now!"

Though he clearly heard the shout, Moonhunter didn't see anyone moving forward as commanded. They didn't look like any of the vehicles possessed anything which could be considered blasters. He also still didn't know why everyone seemed to be in a panic.

"Take it to ground," another voice ordered.

Suddenly, Moonhunter found a large chunk of the caravan heading down toward them.

"Dive," Ralph shouted. "Get out of their way."

"What's causing the panic?" Moonhunter asked, realizing that Ralph might understand what was going on here.

"Rel!"

14

"Rel?" Ralph returned with again as though Moonhunter should know exactly who or what he spoke of. Then Ralph pointed.

Moonhunter saw it then, a large black speck in the sky, and at first he thought it was a dragon. Moonhunter pitched through the fleeing caravan and came out the other side while Ralph screamed at him about Moonhunter's insanity the whole time.

Large gray bullets zoomed through the sky toward the flashing oval. Moonhunter felt the Onesong filled with anger and realized that it emanated from this beast. With horror, Moonhunter realized it was a dragon, though it didn't look like one any more.

The flying bullets stopped and moments later fiery orange shots pelted toward the dragon. It roared as several struck it.

"They're just pissing it off. We best get out of here." Ralph looked anxious.

The beast flew over the Airster, letting Moonhunter get a full view of its underbelly. The usual scales which covered a dragon had been torn away, leaving massive amounts of scar tissue. Its wings had been torn and the amount of savage scar tissue covering them amazed Moonhunter that it could even fly.

Moonhunter listened through the Humline of this world for the dragon's song and his eyes widened. He turned his gaze to Ralph. "What happened to Rel? What torture has he endured here?"

"No one knows for certain. It was a long time ago."

Anger rolled through Moonhunter, though he couldn't say it was entirely his own emotions. Most of it might be coming directly from the dragon. "I think I know now why your planet is doomed."

"Doomed?"

The dragon glided around in a wide turn, a much longer arc than one of his size would normally have to make, and started a descent for the caravan.

"Rocktae shaul!" Moonhunter screamed, waving his arms.

Ralph grabbed the wheel of the Airster. "Hey!"

Having gained the attention of the dragon, Moonhunter continued, "Preymak' vinto da'tae sween."

The dragon's eyes widened and it changed course for them. Moonhunter saw the fire swell within Rel's throat.

Moonhunter grabbed the wheel. "Oh, crap!" He pushed the wheel forward, forcing the Airster into a supreme dive. He heard the engines sputter. A blaze of fire breath shot right over their heads, narrowly missing them while Ralph, screaming, ducked as far down in his seat at the harness allowed him.

"What did you say to it?" Ralph hollered at him.

Moonhunter shrugged. He knew full well that he'd only asked it to land so that they could talk about this situation and obviously the dragon was in no mood to talk. He couldn't say he blamed it, not if it had been so badly injured.

Ralph twisted in his seat and peeked behind them. "Whatever you said, you got its attention. It's chasing us now."

Moonhunter glanced in the rearview mirror and saw Rel awfully close behind them. He opened the throttle for more speed from the Airster.

"I change my mind," Ralph shouted as he turned back around to face forward in his seat and he took a tight grip on the harness. "I don't want to go on an adventure with you."

Moonhunter couldn't help grinning at Ralph.

"No!" Ralph stomped both feet down onto the panel in front of him while he held his hands out on the dash.

"Relax," Moonhunter said as he pulled the Airster out of the dive and soared back into the sky, narrowly missing the trees and ground once before them.

The dragon wasn't as quick to react and smashed into the trees, leaving a long trench behind it. Dirt and smashed branches caught up to the Airster.

"Don't close your eyes," Ralph yelled.

Moonhunter didn't listen even as Ralph grabbed his arm and tried to take the controls. He felt Ralph's movements and not only kept the wheel away from Ralph's grasp, but evaded the missiles all flying toward them. "I said to relax. Your panic blocks me from the Humline."

"The what?"

"Relax," Moonhunter commanded again, once again brushing Ralph's invading hand away from the wheel.

Once Moonhunter felt the dragon's crash settling, he turned the Airster back toward the ground. "Keep an eye on the caravan," Moonhunter ordered. "I must check on the dragon first."

"What? You're taking us closer to that homicidal beast?" Ralph started working at the clasp on his harness. "Let me out way before we get to it."

"You're going to take the Airster and follow the caravan," Moonhunter said. "I'll catch up."

Moonhunter landed the Airster a ways from Rel. "Slide over here and get back in the air." Moonhunter removed the harness and pushed himself onto his seat, then jumped over the side of the Airster.

"How will you catch up?" Ralph asked.

"I just will. Go and don't lose sight of it. Stay low so I'll be able to find you."

"How do you know that you'll be able to catch up?"

Moonhunter blinked down the dragon lids. "I'll be able to see you for several miles. After that, I'll still be able to see the heat trail for a good long time."

"Can't you just follow the caravan that way? Why do I need to follow?"

"Yes, but I might need a mode of transportation to carry someone." Moonhunter turned and began to run toward Rel, whose moans were deepening with pain. He felt the Airster lift behind him and knew he could trust Ralph.

Moonhunter jogged up alongside Rel, his dragon lids down so he could take in the extent of Rel's injuries, which were numerous and made his heart ache at the thoughts of what this dragon had endured. He slowed as he reached Rel's shoulder and he came in closer until he could touch the dragon. "Rel? Rel, do you hear me? My name is Moonhunter. My dragon mother was Vehlka of the Ch'bauldi dragons. This world is in need. I'm here to help you."

Rel's head lifted and swung viciously toward Moonhunter, who jumped back out of reach of the dragon's snapping teeth. "I seek no help from the novihomidraks. Where were they before?"

Moonhunter held a hand out tentatively before him. "Look, I can see that you've been hurt. I'm sorry for what was done to you. Please explain what happened to me so I can right this for you. Is this why the world has been doomed to die?"

"The galaxy it's colliding with has done that. Time is a great equalizer," Rel replied angrily.

It relieved Moonhunter some to know that the dragon hadn't called for retribution. "The Wells are tight, but I think you might still fit through. We came with the help of a Shil'mak not much smaller than you. Do you think you are strong enough to try?"

"I want to see this world disintegrate," Rel snarled.

"I understand your bitterness –"

"You do not!"

Moonhunter jumped back again as Rel clawed over the ground in an attempt to drag himself closer to the novihomidrak. Moonhunter found himself needing to quickly retreat away from Rel.

"Why were you attacking the caravan?" Moonhunter shouted, hoping to distract the dragon.

"Because the Onesong said he was trying to escape."

"Yes!" Moonhunter jumped on the opportunity. The dragon was still connected to the Onesong which meant there was still hope. "Yes, he was. I'm trying to get the scientist, Dr. Melstone, to take him off world before the planet is destroyed. Why don't you help me? We could work together."

"No!"

Moonhunter dodged a spit shot of fire from Rel. The fiery ball slammed against a pine tree and started several branches and the stump on fire.

Rel began to dance with delight. "Let it burn, let it burn," he sang, turning around.

Moonhunter jumped over Rel's tail before it smashed into the burning tree, knocking it down and scattering thick cinders in a wide radius around them.

"Why do you want to keep Dr. Melstone here? What has he done to you?" Moonhunter asked as he raced around the side of the dragon toward Rel's head.

Rel swung to watch Moonhunter. "He created it!"

Moonhunter raised one hand out toward the dragon. "Created what?"

Rel lifted its head and looked up toward the sky. "The thing that lives up there. It jumps from moon to moon, terrorizing planets at night."

Moonhunter glanced up to see a crescent of the moon in the sky above them. Aside from it sounding crazy, Moonhunter wondered if there could possibly be something living on the moon. Most moons had little to no atmosphere compared to the planets they circulated. Those that did usually had gaseous atmospheres, deathly toxic to humans, sickening to novihomidraks. "Why would he do such a thing?"

"He knows about the dragons. That's why the council wants to get him off this world."

"Why?" Moonhunter asked sharply. "If he knows about the dragons and this world is dying soon anyway, why worry about getting him off?"

"Is your connection so weak, novihomidrak, that you cannot see the truth?"

Now Moonhunter patted the air with his other hand, still trying to soothe the angry dragon. "Promise you won't burn me, and let me look." He didn't close his eyes as he usually did with trying to tune into the Onesong, and because he had the distraction of the Humline for this

127

world, it took him a bit longer to actually find the solid energy of the Onesong. "Because it's his daughter they want. He created the beast out of her genetics." The thought rippled through Moonhunter, appalling him so much that for a moment he thought he might retch.

"Now you see the truth."

"That's why they approved Balthier to get the family; they've realized the truth. Dr. Melstone is just a pawn."

"Once the novihomidrak council gets him —"

"Dragon Council?"

"Really, boy? What dragons actually serve on that council?" Rel snapped. "Once the novihomidrak council gets him, what do you think is going to happen?"

Moonhunter shrugged, afraid to postulate even a guess. He still hadn't decided if the dragon was quite mad or if Rel might actually have a point regardless of how insane it sounded. "Why don't you clue this young novihomidrak in?"

Rel rolled his dark eyes.

"You know you aren't getting out through the Wells," Moonhunter realized. "You want to keep that thing on the moon and make sure that it dies here when the galaxies collide. And if you can keep Dr. Melstone here too, you think your problem is over."

Rel sneered, the flesh of his muzzle pulling away from one lengthy, sharp canine tooth. "Took you long enough to uncover my motivation. But now let us return to the council and what they want. On second thought, you stay here and think about it. I have a caravan to eat."

Rel flapped his wings, sending smoke and ash into Moonhunter's face and making him cough.

"Wait!" Moonhunter yelled, trying to keep the dragon on the ground.

The dragon would not be held with words. Rel took to

the sky, his beating wings fanning the flames and scattering them further into the forest. The dragon's heavy, uplifting thrusts pushed Moonhunter to kneel on the ground and curl over his knees from the pressure.

"Damn," Moonhunter whispered to himself when the force of the dragon's takeoff released him. Rel wasn't a huge dragon, but he was strong. Moonhunter stretched, his back cracking and popping as he released the tension he'd had to exert to hold himself against Rel's power.

He blinked down his dragon lids to see how far Rel had gotten in catching up to the caravan. Already the dragon had cleared a good three kilometers.

Sirens whined in the distance. Moonhunter hoped someone had called about the forest being on fire rather than the caravan being under attack again. Either way, Moonhunter could hear Balthier telling him to get the scientist, that was their mission, and to focus on it. Burning trees were not his concern, especially on a planet doomed to be torn to shreds when galaxies collided. When that happened, what good would trees do for the planet then?

Moonhunter extended his wings and took off after the dragon.

Ahead, Moonhunter saw several ships flying in a tight formation toward Rel. They spread out and slowed to a stop as if creating a net. Orange lights lit on weapons the crafts carried.

The Airster Ralph had been piloting diverted from its path and took to the ground. At first, Moonhunter thought the Airster might have been hit, but there were no indications of it, no irregular heat signatures that Moonhunter saw with his dragon vision. All looked normal.

Rel tried to pull in tight behind the caravan, which had now arrived at a hole in the net and was going through.

The vehicles in the caravan were adjusting their positions, making themselves in a perfectly straight line.

If Rel was so anxious to get right of Dr. Melstone, why didn't he just fire breath the whole caravan now? It seemed like Rel had no intention of killing the scientist now.

Moonhunter almost laughed at himself. Rel had been questioning him in order to see if Moonhunter knew why the Dragon Council, or the novihomidrak council as Rel had put it, wanted Dr. Melstone. It was a mystery to the dragon as well.

The last Airster in the caravan struck something and exploded in a fireball of blue shockwaves and orange sparks.

Rel tucked his wings in and dove downward tightly. His tail lashed out while trying to keep him balanced and struck an invisible wall. Electric blue lines snapped around Rel's tail and Moonhunter saw them clawing their way beneath Rel's scales. The dragon howled out in pain.

For the second time today, Moonhunter saw Rel strike the ground, sending up a plume of dirt and trees.

Ralph had known the force field would be there. Moonhunter felt the knowledge zip to him through the Humline.

A bellow rose from the ground below as Rel shifted and raised his head to the sky. Knowing the dragon was okay, save for a bruised ego maybe, Moonhunter flew down to where Ralph had landed the Airster.

"I couldn't get into the caravan to go through," was the first thing that Ralph said as Moonhunter tucked his wings away. He supposed that was true enough.

Moonhunter glanced up with his dragon vision and saw the larger armed crafts moving away from the wall. "Is it something that's always there? What's beyond?"

"A government facility or something. I don't know,"

Ralph snapped back. "Look, they destroyed one of their own back there, the last ship of the caravan. They'd do the same to me or you or the beast. I'm done. You have wings. Use them. It's time to let me get home."

Moonhunter nodded. Yes, Ralph had already put in his service and Moonhunter could see the fear in Ralph's eyes. "Thank you for letting me borrow the Airster. I hope you enjoyed the adventure."

"Yeah," Ralph spat as he shoved the Airster into gear and began to lift off the ground.

Moonhunter watched the Airster turn and fly off. Once again, he was back on his own.

15

Balthier sat at a stainless-steel table in a putrid green room with his cuffed hands between his knees. The cuff's chains ran through a U-shaped bar welded to the table. Balthier kept his arms down, hoping to look non-threatening, but he'd tested that he had enough clearance from the table so he could bring his arms up quickly and grab someone if he needed to. He really hoped he'd get to hit someone in the head.

He had a hard time not looking at the darkened windows around the room. None of them had visible bars on them, so he doubted any of them led directly to the outside. He suspected they were watching him and that he'd be able to see right back through the semi-reflective brown glass to them if he'd put his dragon lids down. He wasn't about to give them any reason to think he wasn't human, but from the sounds he heard whispered beyond the metal door, they already knew that.

He stared at the gray laminate floor beneath the table where a bug, which looked like a cross between a stink beetle and a red ant, tried to haul a bit of crust across the floor. It kept twisting out of the curved mandibles.

How very much like his own situation. He needed to be like the crumb and nimbly escape the captors who held him in their clutches.

Patience, he reminded himself, knowing that he hated having patience. But that's what he'd tell Moonhunter if his pupil were here: have patience. Wait for the police to carry him across the floor, then slip out of their hold and run like hell.

The crust was not lucky enough to have legs.

Balthier straightened in his seat and raised his head as he heard first the chiming of a keyring before the door handle rattled, then clicked. He made sure a hard glare met the person admitted to the room, satisfied as he heard the human's heart speed up.

"A little scruffy to be a novihomidrak, aren't you?" the suited man asked.

Balthier felt himself smile, but didn't know how visible it was beneath his beard. "Refined by your excellent accommodations here," he said.

Amusement reached his shrewd eyes. "Let's see if we can work out an arrangement which will bring you better amenities, shall we?"

That pulled the smile off of Balthier's face, but if the man noticed, it didn't show in his body language as he took a seat across the table and scooted his chair in close.

Unfortunately, the table was bolted to the floor.

Patience, Balthier reminded himself.

The man reached inside his suit jacket and pulled out a folded piece of lined, yellow paper. Slowly, as he spoke, he unfolded it, revealing four quarters made by the creases and writing in each quadrant. "It's been awhile since we saw you last. You were here to retrieve a Dr. Melstone from this planet. Is it correct that he refused to go with you, fought you even, because you wouldn't take his family?" He shook the paper as he held it up slightly in front of him as if to get a better view of the writing.

Balthier crossed his arms over his chest.

Suit gave a little grunt, then rustled the paper again. "Maybe that is a bad question. A little hurtful to the ego, perhaps? Let's try something else." He glanced down at the paper, though Balthier suspected he knew everything that was written on it. "You and your apprentice, Moonhunter, another novihomidrak, have returned to try to get Dr. Melstone and his family this time. Is that correct?"

Balthier said nothing.

This time the man tsked, along with a small shake of his head. "This would be so much easier if you would comply and answer the questions. We would rather reward you than punish you. We might even help you in completing your important mission."

The last statement nearly cracked Balthier's silence, if only to ask why they would be so willing to help with impending doom bearing down on their planet. Why help one man and his family escape when everyone else would die? It seemed to fight against humanity's natural survival instinct.

"Shall we try again? Do you care to answer either of the prior questions?"

Balthier kept his mouth shut, speaking no more than the crust did to the bug.

Suit raised his eyebrows, then sighed. "Very well. Next question: how far are you willing to go to keep Moonhunter safe?"

Fear slammed into Balthier's chest like a hot fist. He instinctively reached out to the Humline to see if Moonhunter was all right.

"I would say that Moonhunter is probably in danger that he doesn't even realize yet, wouldn't you?"

Suit's flat tone assured Balthier that there was no empty threat here.

Balthier shot to his feet. "Release me," he said in the lowest growl he could, though the foreboding hanging over Moonhunter brought a rise to his voice he didn't like. Worse, they knew it.

"If only you would answer my questions," Suit said with another drawn out sigh, "this could be over all ready and you would be free to go."

"Yes, I came to retrieve Dr. Melstone from this world and was unable to because I wouldn't take his family. Yes, I am back with orders to get him and his family. I am obviously willing to go very far to keep Moonhunter safe," Balthier said, practically shouting. "Ask your final question."

The man folded up the note and stuck it back in his jacket pocket. "Your loathing of Shil'mak dragons is well-known. You have lost your own novimather, which frees you to do things that other creatures like yourself would not be able."

Already Balthier didn't like where this was going. These people, whoever they were, knew too much about dragons and novihomidraks.

When Balthier said nothing, Suit continued, "Would you be willing to kill a Shil'mak to keep Moonhunter safe?"

Balthier realized he walked a thin line, a wobbling tightrope threatening to cast him to the ground with no net to catch him. Either answer, yes or no, bore disastrous consequences, and quite probably death sentences.

How could he be like the crust and twist out of these mandibles? Surely they meant to crush him, divide him, and consume him up for the good of continuing their species. Either way, he didn't like the outcomes.

"Come now. We were finally getting somewhere. This isn't a hard choice: Moonhunter's safety for a Shil'mak dragon."

Balthier knew by the twinkle in the man's eyes that a weakness had been found and would be used. Damn. He found himself grinding his teeth together.

"Moonhunter," Suit said, holding one hand palm upward. "Dragon?" He raised the other hand and alternated their height like they were scales.

He'd been warned that Moonhunter would be in danger here. Was it not time that Moon learned how to handle himself? Did he not think his apprentice capable of taking care of himself? But on the other hand, as Suit clearly indicated, it was only a Shil'mak dragon. Had it been a Ch'bauldi dragon, there would have been no contest; his answer would have been a firm no, regardless of what would have happened to Moonhunter.

So, if the only difference lay in the type of dragon involved, did that make him question his own loyalty?

"I see this is a real dilemma for you," Suit said.

"Why do you want a Shil'mak dragon dead?" Considering how much they knew about the dragons and novihomidraks, it seemed likely they knew about the saperes as well. Yet the saperes of this world, or the ones Balthier had seen, worshiped Nefterru. Could this world have two temples to the dragons? A Nefterru and a Shil'mauk? Balthier didn't want to tip his hand about all this knowledge, but he knew it meant one of two things: either the Nefterru saperes wanted a Shil'mak dead for some reason, or someone else wanted to hurt the Shil'mauk saperes. Balthier didn't like either option. "It's pretty hard to hurt a dragon or a novihomidrak. From where I'm sitting, human, both seem pretty unlikely to accomplish."

"Fair enough. You have your questions too, I see." He picked a piece of lint off his jacket sleeve. "I am authorized to answer your question. We seek the Shil'mak's death because the dragon is old and crazy."

"Dragons don't go insane Even Shil'mauks, no matter how unhinged they naturally are."

"This one has."

"Are you a sapere or an operative from the Dragon Council?"

"Not authorized to answer on that question, but I will answer: technically, neither."

"Then who do you work for?"

"That I cannot give you any answer at all."

Balthier went to cross his arms over his chest, but the cuffs wouldn't let him. He stopped where they reached as if that were his intent. "Then I guess you don't want my help."

The man sighed. Balthier was really beginning to hate that breathy sound. Suit started to get up and leaned forward over the table. "Then I guess you don't want our help either. Hope you've trained your apprentice well, not just well enough."

16

Moonhunter walked through the light forest of pine trees. It felt good to stretch his legs. As far as he could tell, Rel hadn't become airborne again. He wondered if the dragon had sustained injuries which kept him from flying. Or was the dragon waiting? Did Rel know that they would be leaving the compound soon?

First, Moonhunter went as close to the force field as he dared. He could feel the energy coming off it from several feet away. He walked around the invisible line trying to see inside, but low hills blocked his vision. He tried flying up and circling around. Dragon wings weren't built for straight up and down flight.

Even with his dragon vision he couldn't see any buildings beyond. Since there were no tracks on the land to follow, for all he knew, the caravan had turned and flown toward the city after crossing this threshold. Frankly, they could have gone anywhere.

Moonhunter circled back toward the government compound, remembering that Rel would probably be patrolling there in case they tried to move Dr. Melstone. Maybe he'd get lucky.

Rather, he saw an Airster approaching the shielding. He listened, spotting a change in the hum it produced as it hovered. It had clearance to get through and while he wasn't entirely certain how the shielding worked, he had to figure that whatever opening the gateway produced must be able to accommodate objects larger than this craft. But did it vary by size depending on who wanted in?

He knew he didn't have time to puzzle all this out.

Tucking his wings in, he plummeted toward the craft. Moonhunter opened his wings as he approached the top, forcing an updraft. He dug his talons into the roof of the aircraft so sharply that they tore through the fiberglass. The craft rocked, destabilizing for a moment until Moonhunter drew his wings close to him once more.

The buzzing sounded overhead. He involuntarily ducked.

Sirens filled the air next. He had only a moment to realize that the shield also reflected the world around it, keeping the insides of the dome a secret. This was like a military base, complete with watchtowers, barracks, and troops running on the ground. Several taller buildings sat in the middle as if secured by its surroundings. A tender heart protected by less vital fodder.

And something he did not expect.

The sensation of a sapere's dragon magic barely had a chance to register before bullets started whizzing at him. He threw his wings up around him, cocooning himself inside.

The Airster began to rock as if trying to throw him off. Moonhunter worked his talons deeper so he could clutch the craft with his fingers. He inadvertently tore one of the holes large enough to partially see through and realized the ground was coming fast upon them.

"Use every advantage you are given," he could hear Balthier's rough voice tell him.

"I'm not an idiot," he muttered back at his own thoughts.

The pilot intended on crash landing. Whoever, or whatever, was onboard could become fodder for the sake of shaking off the novihomidrak.

Did they know what he was or why he was here?

Yes, the Humline responded back to him. They had been waiting, knowing he or the dragon would come.

The craft impacted with the ground, bouncing several times as dirt shot out from each impact. They slid sideways.

Through the holes in the craft, Moonhunter smelled fresh blood, not his own but human.

The pilot had been shot.

Everything in the craft was fodder.

Bullets kept coming. They zipped through the craft below Moonhunter. He felt fewer strike him.

"Okay, okay, already. Can't you see your weapons are doing nothing?" a deep voice boomed. "Quit wasting your ammunition!"

Moonhunter felt the energy approaching. Sapere magic.

As the repetition of shots faded, Moonhunter unfolded his wings, raised his head, and swept his gaze around. He fully expected a red dot to mark his chest.

The sapere drew closer, his hands raised slightly.

Moonhunter felt a snarl on his lips, but he repressed it as best as he could. Considering the sapere bore the markings of a Shil'mak dragon and wore the traditional black garb, Moonhunter understood why he'd felt the sapere's magic so strongly and that he shouldn't be surprised. Chances were good that this was a sapere Rel had created. It would explain the vengeance Rel sought.

The sapere stopped a good distance from the crashed aircraft and bowed. "Welcome, novihomidrak."

Moonhunter pulled his fingers out of the craft with such an effort that his joints cracked. "You would dare to greet me like this, Sapere?" Balthier's advice of never trusting a sapere slammed unwelcomed into his mind, along with the thought that he didn't want to let on that he was only an apprentice. The sapere would have much more respect for a master novihomidrak than an underling.

The sapere gave a shaky laugh as he tentatively glanced back over his shoulders and patted the air with his hands. "Forgive my comrades. They are protective of our secrets here, but have little experience with novihomidraks, such as yourself."

Moonhunter pounced from the back of the craft and stretched his legs and back. He tucked his wings behind him, but didn't put them away in case he had further need of their shielding. Bending to look inside the craft, he confirmed his suspicion that the pilot was already dead. Indeed there was a lot of blood. He noticed it dribbling from holes in the bottom out onto the dirt.

"He called out a distress," the sapere felt the need to explain. "When he saw the wings, he thought Rel had him."

"As if their weapons could do any good against a dragon either."

The sapere slid his foot forward in the dirt as if fighting to make himself move toward Moonhunter. "We must keep Rel out of this at all costs, even with our own lives if necessary. The dragon is quite mad, you know."

Moonhunter decided to put on the arrogant disposition

Balthier had around saperes. He tilted his head slightly, just to make the posture his own. "Dragons aren't known for losing their minds."

The sapere issued a sound that seemed like a cross between a laugh and a hiccup. "Th-that's what the other one said too."

"Other one?"

"The other novihomidrak you crossed through the Wells with."

Balthier. They might very well know that Moonhunter was only an apprentice now. It seemed as if Balthier always notified everyone around them of exactly Moonhunter's learning status.

"Is he here?" Moonhunter asked, not wishing to identify Balthier by name. Who knew what guise Balthier had gone by to throw off his captures.

A flicker of a smile released across the sapere's face before he caught it. He couldn't pull that look back fast enough, but he still pretended that it hadn't happened. "He was brought to the compound, but before you get any grand ideas of rescue, he has been moved on." A pause where once again the sapere struggled with himself. "Moved on to a task more suited to him."

Moonhunter locked his gaze with the sapere and took a steady step forward. "There are five towers with three armed men in each. You know that their weapons are no match for me. How long do you think it would take for me to get to the center of the compound? Novihomidraks' minds are lost more often than dragons. Call it a curse of our creation. How do you know that I am not one of them?"

Now the sapere offered a genuine smile. He raised his hand toward Moonhunter's face. The magic swept away as the sapere pointed, "Because you were the final birth of your dragon mother, Moonhunter, and she blessed you greatly, didn't she?"

Moonhunter let his magic wrap back around him, once again hiding the birthmarks blazoned on his face. Because of those lines, he'd often been mistaken for a child blessed with dragon magic, one who would become a sapere. Balthier encouraged Moonhunter to shield them, keeping them locked behind magic for so long until Moonhunter could do the magic unconsciously and even maintain it while he slept.

He wanted to ask if the sapere had something to make of that, but the sapere continued anyway, "Loved you deeply, she did."

"Yeah, so what? I don't see why that would matter at this moment," Moonhunter said.

The left corner of the sapere's mouth lifted slightly higher than the other, letting the very edges of his teeth show through. "Because those novihomidraks made from love, and make no mistake about it for she loved you before she took you, always have a tender heart." He turned and pointed his finger around at the towers. "There is no way that you could kill all the men up there. It's not in your compassionate heart."

"That almost sounds like a challenge." Moonhunter stepped forward, offering a view of his dragon teeth. "I could start with you."

The sapere stepped back. "I have a better idea. Why don't you come with me and let me show what is so important that we have to guard in this compound? Your mood might change when you see it."

Moonhunter doubted it. "I think I'll take the self-guided tour." He moved around the sapere and started down the compact dirt road.

The sapere's strides opened to catch up with Moonhunter quickly. "You won't find anything," he warned. "Not here at least. This really is just a military compound for this world, a place for key scientists to work without the general population figuring out what they are doing."

"Like Dr. Melstone using his own daughter's genetic code to create a monster? Does the girl even know?"

"Well, how very interesting that you would have heard that rumor already." The sapere paused for a moment and rubbed his finger over his chin. Then he quickly caught up with Moonhunter again. "Is that what you think Melstone was creating here? The Grekish?"

"Since you know its name, then I suspect it's more than a rumor."

Moonhunter came to a building where four men in dark brown uniforms stood before the door, each with a rifle crossing their bodies as they held it in both hands. Their eyes were firm and cold as they watched Moonhunter, who couldn't sense a single drop of fear in them. So confident considering they must have just seen him walk away from a bullet-ridden, crash-landed ship. What could turn a man away from his natural emotions? There had to be some fear as they stood before him, wondering what he would do next. They had to know he could bring their deaths within their next breath.

"Are you truly even a sapere?" Moonhunter asked.

"You would even ask me this after I have taken off your dragon spell to reveal your face and identified you as a pevitias?" The sapere shook his head. "I guess this is why you are still an apprentice."

Moonhunter looked over the wall of men still standing firm before the doorway to the building he wished to enter. He didn't know why he was drawn to this building in particular, but he knew he had to get inside. He trusted being guided like this.

He contemplated pushing a threat of eating the guards to see if that would evoke any emotion from them. It would be simpler to put them all to sleep.

A prickle of tension whizzed up his back. "Very clever, Sapere," Moonhunter said as he reached out and snatched the sapere by the collar of his robes. Just as he yanked the sapere toward him, the four guards emanated bright sparks. Moonhunter leapt into the air. Shots of light chased him. He flapped his wings as they surged after Moonhunter. Two tried to snap around his ankles while the other two missed lassoing his wrists.

He heard the sapere curse behind him. Moonhunter turned his gaze to the height of the building to contemplate landing on the roof. But why go for the obvious when there were so many windows on this building.

Fear went through his stomach. He'd never had a chance to test aerobatics with his wings. Until coming to this planet, he'd hardly used them at all, preferring to keep their existence a secret. He was too close to the window and making an easy turn in the air, one he was sure he could make, would take far longer than a quick flip. But could he do it?

He closed his eyes and saw the maneuver in his mind. He let his body take over, felt himself leaning backwards, then falling.

His wings opened, then he was flying forward again. He struck the glass and crashed through it. The hit to his head slammed pain down his back and shoulders. Shards of the window pelted his wings and he felt them roll, some of them falling away, as he tucked his wings and stretched them once more. He knew the ringing sound wouldn't last long.

People inside shrieked and ducked behind tables. Part laboratory, there were also secretaries typing up notes.

Moonhunter blinked down his dragon lids, knowing that more had to be happening than he was seeing.

Among all the scientific equipment, there ran an electrical stream of energy. It swirled around the room as if it had been captured. Now, it saw the broken window and slithered through the air toward the opening.

"Raise the barrier," a woman shouted. She had a dark, shielding visor wrapped around her head, and little rainbows of light flickered over the smoky surface as she moved to point at the stream.

An alarm sounded as Moonhunter landed. He saw a blue shield go up over the window. The energy stream swarmed around back into the room.

"Someone get him," she then commanded, swinging her pointing finger at Moonhunter.

Most of the scientists, and those huddled close to take notes, didn't seem to want to charge after him. He kept his dragon lids down, knowing that most of them would be frightened off by the odd inhuman look of their red color. But there were guards too who didn't seem to be threatened by him. He extended his dragon teeth, grinning. That didn't seem to bother them much either.

They knew what he was.

A man raised a gun.

There was an oily black sheen to it. Novihomidrak forged.

The shot fired.

The beam of energy intercepted the bullet. Moonhunter heard the projectile clink on the floor. He kept going for the door, not looking back.

Steam came out from floor and ceiling vents, surprising Moonhunter. It wasn't so much hot as it was moist. The smell of disinfectants surrounded him. Then the glass door ahead of him slid open.

"Would someone lock this floor down?" he heard the woman shout behind him. "Does anyone know what that means?"

Slow, rotating yellow lights in the hallway changed to blaring red which strobed against the white walls. Moonhunter found himself dizzy. He collapsed against the wall.

The energy followed him, coming up alongside him as if urging him to keep moving. The only hope it had for escape was with him.

He nodded his understanding and pushed away from the wall. Blinking away the dragon lids helped a little, but the on and off of the lights made his movements feel staggered and disjointed.

"Which way?" he called out to the energy, hoping it could be a guide though he could no longer see it. He could sense it though, moving beside him. Balthier had always refused to believe the energy running through everything, regardless of his knowledge of the Onesong and how many Humlines he had touched, but Moonhunter had seen energy worked by masters. It had given him a different perspective than his mentor.

The energy surged ahead and turned down a branching hallway.

The mechanic sound of bolts sliding into locked position chased them. The energy kept going, but Moonhunter felt a deep need to open one of the doors before it locked. He reached out as he rushed by a door and pushed it open. Another turn and they came to another laboratory. Moonhunter ran across close enough to engage the sensor. The door slid open and the disinfectant sprayed out. Moonhunter raked his talon across the doorframe, shredding the metal so the door wouldn't slide closed again.

He pushed himself harder, feeling the sound of the locks getting ahead of him.

The energy zipped between the central seam of a set of elevator doors. He saw the light go on for the elevator to open.

Then he heard the bolt engage from the floor. The door banged against it, but didn't open. The light changed from a cheery green to a bright, mocking red.

A man ran out of the clean room where Moonhunter had clawed the door. "What is going on here?"

Moonhunter felt ancient magicks swirling around him as his chest filled with air. He focused, and when he spoke, his voice rumbled deeply. "Nothing is happening. You will turn off the alarm and go back to work."

The man's eyes went blank as if he didn't even see Moonhunter any longer. He did a quick search of the hallway, then went back to his lab.

Moonhunter didn't trust the alarm would just stop or that the people from the first room would quit chasing him. For a moment, he wished he had the fire or acid breath he knew some novihomidraks possessed. He still had only three choices: go up, go down, or go back. Would any of the rooms where he'd left the doors open yield him an escape?

Moonhunter ran back to the previous lab. The disinfectant mist still spewed from the vents. Holding his breath, he walked into the room. He looked for the man who had come running out into the hallway and found him standing over his experiment while others in the room seemed scattered, disorganized, and confused. Several of them startled when Moonhunter entered.

He blinked down his lids, wondering if there was another beam of energy in here. There didn't seem to be. Of course, it might have already fled for freedom. Or it wasn't attuned to him. Or whatever else energy could do which he wasn't aware of.

"Man to whom I've already spoken, what are you doing here?" he asked, directing his command so that he wouldn't get a jabber of information from everyone in the room all at once.

The scientist looked up from his work while nearly everyone else in the room turned their gazes to him as if wondering at his answer. "We are tracing the hierarchy energy and making a map of it."

"Where is this energy coming from?"

"Why, the convergence of course."

"What's the convergence?"

Moonhunter's question broke several of the people from their trances. Some went for the scientist, tackling him. Others came for Moonhunter. He turned with a growl, "Is there an emergency exit from this lab?"

The nearest person fell under his enthrall and pointed toward a cupboard in the back corner.

"Where will it take me?"

"To the roof or to the basement. Hit the button to select your destination," the man answered.

"Where will I find the convergence?"

"Behind the sparkling door."

That wasn't much information to go on, but Moonhunter knew he didn't have long enough to press for more information. He could feel the novihomidrak forged weapons drawing closer to his location.

Moonhunter pushed through the people trying to surround him and made it to the back corner. It worried him a little that in the ensuing chaos no one had tried to get over here. Was this really a trap? If it wasn't an emergency exit, was it made to hold a novihomidrak, or just an ordinary human?

He could just break the window and fly to another level.

As tempting as that idea seemed, he felt himself being urged against it. He opened the door to the cabinet and found a padded room little bigger than a dumbwaiter. He'd fit quite snuggly in it. Obviously it was only meant for one person. So much for an escape route if only one person could leave at a time.

No, it was meant for only the lead scientist to get out. Everyone else was expendable.

Before Moonhunter could even wonder who the lead scientist was, he knew: that man had already escaped, probably as the initial alarm sounded.

He tucked himself in and pulled the door shut behind him. Just as the man had said, there were two stacked buttons in front of him, neither labeled. He pushed the one for the basement.

The intense drop put his stomach in his throat.

The elevator stopped as if it landed upon a cloud. The door swooshed open, revealing a cement room lit with florescent tubes running along the roof.

He stepped out, his senses on high alert, especially as the lights above him flickered and buzzed. A chill circled his chest and ran down along his arms. Another scent, one of a human, lingered like a fresh spray on the odor of dank, stale air. Moonhunter stepped around the corner of the elevator to look further into that section of the room.

The sapere from outside leaned against the wall, his arms crossed. "I figured you'd be arriving soon," the sapere said.

"You did, huh? Why's that?"

The sapere pushed away from the wall. "Because they always show up here eventually. Your time is about average."

17

The man in the clean, dark suit leaned over the stainless steel table toward Balthier, effectively blocking the grayish mint green walls. Balthier noticed the scent of magic on the man as well as something else. With a deeper breath, Balthier tried to identify it. Earthy, almost like dirt, but one glance at the man's smooth hands and clean, clipped nails didn't show any indication of even light work like gardening.

How did a clean-shaven man in an immaculate three-piece suit pick up the scent of earth on him? He had to be surrounded by it. An underground facility? But even then, the walls would keep the dirt back and conditioned air filtered and piped in, so that wouldn't cause this type of scent.

"Is Moonhunter trained well enough to protect himself, or have you sheltered him and kept him from understanding the true nasties in throughout the universe?" Suit asked.

Balthier forced himself to remain quiet. If he caved now, Suit would know he had the upper hand. He gave a little shrug as if he didn't care, but he still looked to the Humline to check on Moonhunter's safety.

"You know..." Suit settled back in his chair and shifted slightly as if preparing for round two of difficult negotiations, "...there's a little thing that you abominations do when you do whatever it is you're doing now that's a big tell. Your eyes shift ever so subtly. It's like they almost flatten for a moment. I've even had your kind try to stop the action, but it never works. It's a very curious feature because it's almost like it's instinctual."

Balthier realized this man was trying to get a rise out of him. Only once in their conversation had Suit said "creatures," and all other times it had been "novihomidraks" until now. But Suit hadn't left the table and had no intention of leaving the room. Suit wanted something and these wrangling tactics were designed to test Balthier's strengths and weaknesses. He might as well oblige.

"Hey, I thought it was simple." Balthier gave another shrug. "You tell me who you work for and we get to an agreement. I've got to know where to send the bill."

Suit thought about this for a moment, his face unreadable and without a flicker of emotion. Balthier wondered if there was some brainwashing involved. Or maybe implants which allowed another person to watch and decide what happened from behind the scenes. Someone from this planet who knew that his life were about to end soon might go to extraordinary lengths to preserve himself, even to the point of allowing himself to be used as a puppet. That might also explain the misplaced, earthy odor.

"Are you really willing to make a deal outside of the Dragon Council's approval?" Suit asked.

Fear coiled inside Balthier's chest; the answer could get him imprisoned. A novihomidrak locked up in a facility was the worst thing he could imagine. Yet, Moonhunter's safety might be on the line. "Yes. I do it quite often." Balthier's eyes darted with the confession regardless of him trying to keep them steady.

The man opened up his file once more. "You didn't have an easy time of your early novihomidrak years, did you? Seems your mentor took more delight in assaulting you rather than training you. Is that correct?"

Balthier tried desperately to read what was on the paper before Suit, but upside down and in a language foreign to him, the task was impossible.

"Doesn't matter what it says," Balthier said finally. "I suspect you knew about my reputation and the kind of deals I make before coming to this little meeting. Aren't we negotiating what it will take to free me from this confinement and get me out there taking down a dragon?"

Suit closed the file, but set his hand down on it. "This is part of the negotiation. You see..." He tapped his finger against the file. "I'm betting that a lot of what's in here about your past, neither the Dragon Council nor many of the Ch'bauldi saperes are aware of it."

"Hard to say. I don't know what you've got written in there." Balthier tried to look unimpressed. Every bit of information Suit leaked out filled Balthier with grueling unsettlement.

"Do the saperes know that you were... oh, how is it phrased in here..." He opened the file and dragged his finger across the page until he found what he was looking for. "Yes, here it is: 'beaten like a dragon-skinned punching bag'?"

Balthier took deep breaths, fighting against the fiery blood slamming through his heart. His anger boiled just beneath the surface, but he really wanted to know who had gained this information on him. He doubted this file was with Suit alone, which meant there were additional copies of it somewhere.

"Why you?" Suit asked suddenly. "Why did your novimather choose you to mentor her pevitias?"

"I don't know." The words felt like grit in his mouth. He'd often wondered the same thing. All he knew was that mentoring Moonhunter had been the best thing in his life and had restored his abused hope in the universe.

He had always taken it as a sign that he'd cleared up some of his karma, that the Onesong approved of the new choices he'd made in his life. But now, with Suit sitting across from him, he had to wonder if he'd been living in the eyes of the storm for the last few years.

"You've kept everything about your past from Moonhunter. He doesn't know much about you, does he? Certainly none of this." Suit pointed at the file. "But don't you think he senses it, that wall you have up? What if he has his own wall? Does he have secrets from you as well? If you'd been open and honest with him, then he might never have felt the things you keep from him, making him choose to do the same."

Balthier thought about Moonhunter always saying that he was meditating in his room. He'd always felt there was more than what Moonhunter said.

"There it is. Yes, you do know it," Suit said in a smug tone as he leaned back and crossed his arms triumphantly over his chest. "In case you are wondering, it's always been a mystery to us too why your dragon mother chose you. Vehlka had her reasons and they were hers alone."

Us? Who was Suit talking about?

"I hope that gives you some comfort," Suit continued, "knowing that your novimather specifically chose you for the task of mentoring Moonhunter."

Balthier held every emotion in his chest, it feeling

strange to do so again after so many years. He really didn't want Suit to suspect how much the words were affecting him. He wished he knew if he was being successful at this, though he also believed his silence was saying more than any flicker of emotion across his face would.

"I am from the Wellsdeep." Suit proclaimed this as if Balthier's hearing it would make everything crystal clear.

Balthier continued to stare dryly at Suit.

Something akin to a wry smile lit across Suit's face. "I guess there are some things which are kept even from the underbelly of the Onesong. I am really surprised. I would have thought a novi with your seedy background would know about the Sanctuary. Why have you never shared any of your shady past with Moonhunter? Don't you think he has a right to know what goes on out there and what he's really up against?"

"I wish you wouldn't talk about me with words like seedy and shady. I didn't have a choice back then, and when I finally did, I didn't always know better. If you think the travesties humans normally do to each other is horrific, imagine what they will do to someone who seems immortal. Moonhunter doesn't need to know about that."

Suit's face became more serious than Balthier had seen him so far in this conversation. He leaned forward with his elbows on the table. "My father tried to get you out. Wellsdeep knew what was going on. He died... died regretting that he couldn't get to you."

"So it didn't do either of us any good!" Balthier jerked against his restraints, making metal chains clank against the restraining loop. "He was obviously a fool to go against the Onesong. I knew that what was happening to me, every punch, every rape, every stabbing was building me into someone. It was destined to be. Don't come in here now and tell me there was someone out there trying to save me.

I don't want to hear it, or his excuses as to why he failed." He slammed his hands against the edge of the table.

"I just thought you should know."

"May it soothes your conscious, because it doesn't mine."

Suit waited, as if giving Balthier time to calm down. He kept looking like he wanted to add something, but wisely kept his mouth shut. Then, apparently when he'd decided that Balthier was no longer going to rip his face off, something even Balthier wasn't certain he'd given up on, Suit folded his fingers together and once again placed them on top of the file. He continued to sit in silence for a little longer.

Finally, he said, "I should start at the top. Let's talk about Wellsdeep." He paused, his lips pulling in tightly at the corners. It gave Suit the look as if he'd smelled something foul. "Wellsdeep is the heart of the Onesong. It crosses dimensions so that it exists in every planet connected to the Onesong. Right now, because of what is going on here with the Shil'mak dragon, Wellsdeep is severely threatened. I am one of the Wellsdeep Keepers. My name is Ralph."

18

The florescent lights of the basement buzzed and flickered, making the greenish-gray walls darken to a blue hue every time it dimmed. It stabilized, leaving the approaching sapere drenched in unnatural light. It made the sapere appear pale and sickly especially in contrast to the black Shil'mak robes.

For the most part, this basement room seemed unused. There were metal shelving units with wide gaps to fit the rather large boxes which were on them. A couple of the shelves had boxes stacked two or three high on the floor in front too. If the labeling on the boxes were true, it was additional food and medical supplies. For all Moonhunter knew, they were merely empty boxes. He really couldn't trust anything here, and certainly not the sapere strolling toward him.

The sapere's black hair had become disheveled in his hurry to beat Moonhunter to the basement, all so he could stand here now claiming that Moonhunter had arrived right on time.

Moonhunter gaped at the sapere standing before him. "Average?" Moonhunter asked.

The sapere gave a snort. "Yes, average. But, since the other novihomidraks trying to get down here were masters, maybe you should be proud. You're the first apprentice to make it here."

Moonhunter looked around. "And where exactly are we other than a basement. I've seen a few of these before. This isn't anything special."

"Then maybe you need to look harder, young novihomidrak."

Moonhunter sighed and blinked down his dragon lids. The moment he opened his eyes, a flash of pain went through his head. Light so bright shined in his head that it felt as if it were going right through him. He winced, scrunching his eyes closed tightly. He opened them again without his dragon lids and found himself blind.

The sapere took his arm.

"What have you done?" Moonhunter growled.

"A necessity. Hold still. This will all be over in a moment."

Moonhunter listened for someone else to approach, fully expecting an attack. The sapere's hand never left him. He felt magic. It spun through him like a whirlwind.

"I know it's not comfortable," the sapere whispered to him. "Stay calm."

"You give me no reason to be calm, sapere," Moonhunter rumbled. "What is going on?"

"An explanation."

"It had better be a good one, and one that I want."

"I think you will find yourself amazed," the sapere said. His hands left Moonhunter as the sensation of magic dwindled away too. "Open your eyes and view with your dragon lids once more. I apologize for the pain. It was necessary for your safety."

Moonhunter almost preferred the blackness compared to the pulsing white that lit his sight as he did as the sapere requested. He shut his eyes tightly once more. "You realize that not much can hurt a novihomidrak, right? I would worry about your own safety rather than mine."

"Ordinarily that is true enough, but not where we have gone."

Gone? If they had left the basement, then Moonhunter needed to assess the new surroundings and quickly.

Moonhunter blinked opened his eyes. "Where have we gone?" As his sight cleared, he saw they were still in the basement. Before he had a chance to ask the sapere what sort of trick this was, a door materialized before him.

But the door itself didn't fit here, in the basement of concrete, as it was wood and wrought iron surrounded with a brick frame. It blurred where it met the concrete. Little, green vines appeared right out of the concrete and clung to the reddish brick.

"Dimensional magic?" Moonhunter asked.

"Not quite."

"Energy work then?"

"Your adventures have indeed been extensive, haven't they?" The sapere gave an impressed nod. "Come. Why don't we take a deeper look?" He ran his hand over the door and glyphs lit on the wood, shining in the same green as the vines on the wall. From just beyond the door, Moonhunter heard gears begin to turn. A moment later, the writing turned bright yellow. A soft click accompanied the change and the door opened of its own accord.

A blue glow and the damp scent of cavernous earth slipped from beyond and assaulted Moonhunter's senses. He involuntarily growled.

"It might help if you showed it you were a true pevitias," the sapere suggested as he pulled the door open, exposing a long tunnel which closely resembled those going out to the underground swimming pools where he'd gone with his friends, Serchk and Sundancer. "Tell the Wells who you are."

Moonhunter noticed that the sapere had collected a spear somewhere along the way, possibly when Moonhunter had been blinded. The tip of the spear was unmistakably from the tail of a shock dragon. Was that how the sapere intended on keeping Moonhunter in line? Most body parts of the shock dragon could inflict a lot of pain, but the electrical power drained quickly out of them. The spiky tip of the tail lasted the longest, but Moonhunter suspected that he was youthful enough to withstand the shock until it dulled.

With luck, the sapere knew that the weapon also wouldn't last long against Moonhunter if the sapere wanted to start a fight. He didn't want a battle to be held here.

The sapere repeated his gesture for Moonhunter to speak. Moonhunter took another step forward, looking through the doorway toward the tunnel. "I am Moonhunter, novihomidrak to Vehlka of the Ch'bauldi dragons."

Nothing seemed to happen until Moonhunter noticed the sapere gaping at him and he asked, "What?"

"Did you not feel it?"

Moonhunter looked around as if that would help him to sense whatever the sapere referenced. "Feel what?"

The sapere looked around in awe, a smile widening on his face. "The collective breath that the Wells took." His eyes met once again with Moonhunter's. "Once you've attuned your magic with the Wells, you are going to be amazed."

This sapere was so self-assured and certain that Moonhunter would meekly submit to his biddings. It annoyed Moonhunter and he now understood why Balthier distrusted the saperes so much.

"Come, come, I will show you." The sapere hurried on ahead and opened up another door. "You will see and there are many wonders."

Considering how deeply underground they seemed to be, Moonhunter expected catacombs in the other room. Instead, he walked into a huge cavern where a draft swirled from a long cylindrical opening above. He couldn't even see the top of it.

Moving forward, the sapere's arm stopped him and brought Moonhunter's gaze back to his immediate surroundings. A tall wrought iron fence surrounded a gaping hole before him. A short path led down a slope of the ravine to a bridge, which looked like a toothpick silhouetted in the white-blue light coming from beneath it. Moonhunter stepped up to the ancient fence, wrapping his hands around the twisted iron poles. The age of it sang to him, filling him with nearly as much awe as the sight of this space did.

The sapere motioned him on. "You are beginning to understand. Let us go out on the bridge where you may see more of its expanse."

"Why are you showing me this?" Moonhunter's fingers tightened on the rail as if the metal could give him the answer he feared the sapere would deny him. "Why me?"

"Beyond the fact that you are a pevitias?"

"Yes. There has to be more."

"Your answers will come. But for now, examine what is before you, young novihomidrak."

The sapere wound down a track that seemed invisible to Moonhunter, but he could tell that the sapere had moved down ample times before. The metal railing turned to a loosely hung chain. Moonhunter's boots slipped on the slimy rocks, drenched by mossy time. He snatched onto the chain and held tightly as he made his way down after the sapere who he thought he heard chuckle softly.

As they got closer to the bridge, the white-blue glow brightened until Moonhunter shielded his eyes with his hand. He didn't know why it didn't bother the sapere.

His foot skated out from beneath him once more. He fell, skidding down the rocks. His fingers snatched out for the chain. Missed. Talons came out, digging into the green covered rocks. Dewy moss tickled against his skin. His grip wouldn't hold.

Moonhunter's wings sprouted and pushed him up with a flap, enough that he could grab the chain. The sapere reached over and helped Moonhunter up, and then steady himself on his feet. Moonhunter marveled at the sapere's strength.

"Careful now," the sapere admonished.

Moonhunter nodded.

The sapere headed out onto the bridge. Being closer now, it seemed much larger than it had from above. The metal tolled beneath the sapere's feet, sounding like a deep wind chime which echoed through the tunnel. The sapere looked over the solid wall of the bridge which came up to his mid-chest to prevent him from falling over. Moonhunter thought that the railing down to the bridge should have been similarly crafted rather than a single chain.

Of course, then it wouldn't be a very effective trap to keep someone who wasn't supposed to be there off the bridge. Because of his wings, he was meant to be there. The sapere had learned the proper steps down to the bridge, something that could be taught over the ages, but Moonhunter could fly and didn't even need the path.

Moonhunter blinked down his dragon lids and took a sweeping glance around to see if he'd missed anything else. Nothing came immediately. He stepped out onto the metal bridge and looked down. His wings gave an involuntary flap even as his breath caught in his throat.

He'd never stood overlooking a hole so deep.

Even with his dragon vision, he couldn't see the bottom.

"What is this?" he asked the sapere.

The sapere frowned as he gazed over the bridge with Moonhunter. "You are looking at Wellsdeep."

"Wellsdeep? What is that?"

The frown deepened as if disappointed that Moonhunter didn't comprehend everything from the word alone. "This is the dimensional convergence for the birthplace of worlds."

Moonhunter surveyed the length of the round walls in both directions as far as he could see each way. "Wellsdeep," he whispered, letting the word resonate through him and hoping for the Onesong to provide information he needed. He glanced back at the sapere. "I'm still not sure I understand."

Without holding onto the railings, the sapere moved further out onto the bridge as if he'd done it hundreds of times before. "Every space you see in the wall is a doorway. Each one has a window that lets us watch the worlds growing beyond."

"Why?" Moonhunter asked, knowing he needed more information. "Why would the saperes need to watch the worlds?"

"Why would we not? You know how this came into being, don't you?"

Moonhunter stared all around, seeking an answer, but ended up shaking his head.

The sapere's mouth slacked. "Do you not feel it? You helped an imagination dragon. Do you not understand what they do?"

"The stardust orb," Moonhunter said flatly. "No, I never knew what happened to it after I turned it over to the sapere. Balthier said it was best that I forget about it."

The sapere returned a soft smile. "Trust me. Stardust, as the dragon decided to call himself, and Reila are enjoying many adventures. She will, in time, become Stardust's first Wellskeeper."

"Wellskeeper?"

"That is what we are called, saperes who watch over the many worlds created by an imagination dragon. Here, we are called the Wellsdeep Keepers because, well, this is Wellsdeep."

Moonhunter felt dense and knew he was missing a large piece. "I still don't understand what this place is or how imagination dragons fit in."

"Imagination dragons create all the worlds. They all come here to Wellsdeep to begin. They thrust through the wall and begin building their own worlds. Wellsdeep is a fold in time and space, and a place of dreams given birth," the keeper said.

"You mean each window up there is really where an imagination dragon has gone through and that the many galaxies on the Wells are…" Moonhunter could barely fathom the expanding thought that came to him as there were no words for it. No, there was only the final realization. "This is the internal structure of the Wells."

The sapere's smile grew. "Yes."

"This is the main trunk of the Wells then. Each one of the windows is an off-shoot. The imagination dragon creating the branch makes his own Wellskeepers, but they all report back to the Wellsdeep Keepers because this is the stem of all life."

"Yes."

Moonhunter felt his legs weaken beneath him.

"It's okay to sit down on the bridge if you need to. I remember how overwhelming this can be."

Gripping the railing, Moonhunter fought to not let his spinning head get the better of him. "What do you want with me? Why am I here?"

"You are here because you are a pevitias and you have helped an imagination dragon. One of those things marks you for great things, but to have accomplished both makes you a rare breed. We brought you here because you must understand what you are fighting for."

Moonhunter glanced around again. "Look, I'm here to help Balthier get Dr. Melstone and his family off this planet before it experiences the gravitational destruction of the two galaxies colliding. Wellsdeep doesn't appear to be in any danger. In fact, it's downright peaceful here. Beyond that, I know my mission as a novihomidrak is to keep chaos at bay. I'm well versed in what I need to do."

"Did I mention that I know you are attempting the Crossing? A pevitias who has helped an imagination dragon, and taken on all his aspects to become the ultimate creature that he could possibly be... well, that would be truly a remarkable and unique novihomidrak."

The sapere's words chilled Moonhunter and he couldn't believe he'd let himself be led down here so easily. It wouldn't be hard for someone to make a sacrifice of him right here. "Take me back," Moonhunter growled, his voice deep and possessed. "I must return to my mission."

The sapere laughed. "Oh, believe me, your mission is here. I just need to make you see it."

Moonhunter couldn't believe the sapere so easily shook off the dragon magic. He let the spur of anger fuel his second attempt. "Take me back. I will finish my mission."

Looking humored, the sapere crossed his arms over his chest. "Your mission is here. I promise you. What you look for, you will find in Wellsdeep."

The caravan had been traveling toward the base and had gone through the shield. Yes, Dr. Melstone was here. "Where is Dr. Melstone?"

"I believe I am the one you are seeking," a voice said behind him.

Moonhunter whirled around to see a gray haired gentleman standing in sapere robes. "Dr. Melstone?"

"That's right."

"You're a Wellsdeep Keeper too?"

"I am. That is why I cannot leave this planet. I hope you understand. I hope I can convince you to stay as well."

Moonhunter thought about the colliding galaxy. Didn't Dr. Melstone realize that the gravitational forces would soon start to rip this planet apart?

He waved his hand. "I know what you are thinking. This planet is doomed. We must get all the saperes off and save as many lives as we can. Have you felt any hurt over the ones that we won't be able to save? Of course you have. You're one of the good novihomidraks. That is why we have brought you here. Why Balthier had to be separated from you."

Moonhunter gripped onto the rail, resisting the little part of himself urging him to jump and let his wings fly him to safety. Yet he felt a large part playing out before him and leading him into unknown territory. These Wells were old and the ancient souls calling to him bade for his cognizance. He needed deep understanding of what was happening here. "Balthier is my mentor. Why did you need him away?"

"He's not like you, Moonhunter. His soul is tainted by heavy darkness. He's done some terrible things in his life."

Moonhunter wanted to deny it but couldn't. He's knew Balthier cloaked secrets from him. But Moonhunter had kept his own desire to accomplish the Crossing from Balthier. Everyone had a right to change themselves. Just as Moonhunter wanted to become a better novihomidrak, Balthier's shield let him become a better human. "So why am I here?"

Dr. Melstone stepped out on the bridge. His comfort of walking on the dangling metal showed in that he didn't even lay a hand on the railing. "We want you to become a Wellskeeper."

With an unsteady step backwards, Moonhunter's awareness spread to moving closer to the other sapere behind him on the suspension bridge.

"I see your apprehension," Dr. Melstone said gently. "I had hoped that if we showed you all this, you would understand what we are protecting here. We have all made sacrifices in order to guard Wellsdeep." His words held calm distance, but sadness touched his eyes at the thought of the daughter he'd lost. "We give up things in order to be the palladium of the larger universe. Surely you can understand that. Your novimather sacrificed her own life to make sure you were born. Is it not time to repay that gift?"

"I'm not ready," Moonhunter answered. "I have been quested to bring you back to the Dragon Council. Maybe if you came with me to visit the Council, it would give us time to talk and I could understand what it is that you do here. Right now, where I stand, I don't see that my novimather would want me to stand still just to protect the

Wells. I feel that she would want me out helping the people of many worlds to have better lives."

"Do you want to become your best novihomidrak self?"

"Very much."

"We can aid you with the Crossing."

Temptation nearly swayed him as much as the bridge beneath him as the sapere moved up behind him. He heard a soft chant being spoken and felt it worming over him as if lulling his wings to emerge from his back. Moonhunter fought to control all his dragon aspects.

"See how much your novihomidrak side wants this?" Dr. Melstone spoke.

"Why are you still trying to persuade me? I told you that I wasn't ready. We need to go back to the Dragon Council."

"Don't you understand? That was merely the way to get you here."

"But Balthier failed this mission the first time."

"Yes, he did. We hoped his bad history would leave him desperate and angry. Once he was here, we saw he wasn't strong enough to defeat the Grekish, so we sent him home in disgrace."

"You keep implying that Balthier is weak and traumatized, but he isn't. He's been a great mentor."

Dr. Melstone scoffed. "Even you sense his weakness or you would have shared your plans for the Crossing with him. Take a look around. Is this not the greatest thing you have ever seen? We want you to be part of all this. We can help you achieve the secret dreams hidden in your heart, and you know we are capable of that. Balthier has reached the end of his usefulness for you."

A shadow moved under Moonhunter. Far beneath him, a dragon flew through the Wells. Moonhunter watched its flight and admitted that it was the most awe-inspiring thing he'd ever seen. For just a moment, he allowed himself to think about being out on this bridge every day watching the dragons soaring around him. But standing still wasn't the life Vehlka wanted for him. Maybe Balthier had committed wrongs in the past, but Vehlka had thought him to be the right mentor for her pevitias. She wanted to correct the wrongs behind Balthier and Balthier had walked that path ever since. Moonhunter had been that bridge for Balthier to cross.

Balthier had always told him to never trust a sapere, that they always had their own agenda with the dragons. He doubted that Balthier even knew about this sanctuary.

"Why are you doing this?" Moonhunter found himself asking suddenly. "You all are saperes. Why do you really want a novihomidrak here?"

Dr. Melstone looked disappointed. "Not any novihomidrak; a pevitias and the one we could save."

"I don't understand."

"It is not the colliding galaxies that endanger these Wells, but rather the Grekish. It must be destroyed. We still want to send Balthier after the Grekish. He has grown and has something to fight for now: you. It is our hope that he can defeat the Grekish, but should he fail, we will vanish once more within the Wells and keep you safe."

"I'd rather fight at Balthier's side. Two of us have a much better chance of defeating this thing than just one."

"Yet if you fail, we lose not only two novihomidraks but a pevitias, and the Grekish will return. It always tracks us down. Do you want to put more planets in peril? Having you with us will get the attention of the dragons who no longer care about their worlds and will enlist their help against the Grekish. Make the choice to stay."

"But if we defeat the Grekish, then it all ends now. Is that not the preferable option?"

"Why can't you be reasoned with?" Dr. Melstone shouted.

"Because there's no logic in your words. Why not bring ten or fifteen novihomidraks here to fight the Grekish? Why not tell the Dragon Council that you need their help?"

Dr. Melstone had gone white with fear. Something about Moonhunter's questions struck a wall that Dr. Melstone didn't want to answer.

The air around Moonhunter rang with the doctor's motives. "You created the Grekish. You don't really want it killed. You want it controlled and you think the answer is a pevitias."

"You're right and your wrong. I didn't create the Grekish; it is a demon of chaos. There is no controlling the Grekish. It follows me from world to world to remind me of my offenses. Every branch of the Wells which it seals makes it stronger. The Grekish must be destroyed to keep the Wells safe."

Hearing this from Dr. Melstone and feeling the urgings of the Onesong, Moonhunter felt his anger rise. "You would sentence Balthier for his past and send him out there to die at the hands of your curse even though it proves your own misdeeds."

"I had really hoped you would understand." Dr. Melstone gave a wave of his hand as he turned and started to walk from the bridge. "Send him."

"Wait. Let's make a plan—" Moonhunter's words got cut off as pain jabbed into his side and electricity coursed through his body. He dropped to his knees. The metal clanged beneath him and an echo rang up through the chamber. Moonhunter tried to twist to see what the sapere behind him speared into him, but he suspected he knew the answer: the long spike from a shock dragon's tail.

Pain caused Moonhunter's eyes to roll back in his head. He felt consciousness leaving him, no matter how hard he clung to it. A fearful thought of them tossing him over the side of the bridge into the tunnel surged a longing to fight, but he was already too far gone. He felt himself fall forward, but never felt the metal greet him. His world went black before that.

B althier listened for the clatter that had gone through the base. It had long been silent, but he still felt Moonhunter's energy nearby.

Ralph came back in the room. "It's official. Moonhunter made it down to Wellsdeep. He's probably spoken to Dr. Melstone by now."

"What do they want with him?" Balthier asked, holding as much of the concern from his voice as he could.

"Probably to go after the Grekish, I would imagine."

Balthier's lips stuck dryly together, the skin pulling on his mouth, as he went to speak the next obvious question. "What's the Grekish?"

"Depends on who you ask."

"I'm asking you."

Ralph shrugged. "Well, then, technically, the Grekish is my cousin."

"What?"

"Did you never wonder why Dr. Melstone didn't want to go with you?"

"He didn't want to leave his family." But as Balthier

spoke the words, he felt the lie within it vibrating back to him through the Humline. "You're Dr. Melstone's nephew."

Ralph sat down and leaned forward over the table separating them. "Do you know how rare it is for Wellsdeep Keepers to be from the same family? This is not a lineage position. It's unusual enough for dragons to make saperes from relatives, but for them to go on and be given honored positions is unique. Almost like having a novihomidrak who is a pevitias and is in the debt of an imagination dragon. Oh so very unusual."

Balthier didn't want the conversation to turn to Moonhunter. He needed information, not anger. "So you and your uncle are Wellsdeep Keepers?"

"As was my cousin. We were a very exceptional family."

"What happened to her?"

Ralph looked down at the table. "Well, you see, that's just it. When you came the first time and he refused to go, Shellee came down here to get her father. She wanted to tell him that you were close. Do you remember?"

"You must have been a teenager then."

"I was, and Shellee not much older. She had just become a Wellsdeep Keeper and I was hopeful I'd be there in a couple more years." Ralph ran flat palms over the table. "Do you remember what happened?"

"I do."

Ralph gave him a glance, then got up for a paper cup. Filling it with water, he slid it in front of Balthier. "I meant what I said. My father did try to save you. And how were you to know that in trying to save Dr. Melstone, it would risk the life of his eldest child? Now's not the time to get choked up."

Balthier gasped, his cheeks filling with air and the

sound exploding from his mouth. "What happened to your cousin?"

"She came running into the Wells. My uncle was working on one of his experiments. The dark matter reached out, grabbed Shellee, and pulled her in. That's when the Grekish was born. If my uncle… if he hadn't been in mourning over my father, his brother, he might have been able to take care of the beast while it was weak and adapting to the humanity it had just discovered."

"I'm sorry."

"Excuse me? What was that?" Ralph asked. "A noviho-midrak apologizing for his actions?"

"Yes. I'm sorry."

Ralph slapped the table. "I could almost believe that. But somehow, I doubt you know the wreckage you made of our lives."

"I failed. The Humline told me I had botched the mission beyond repair. I fled."

"Did you even tell the Dragon Council what happened?"

"Yes."

"Then how did you end up with a pevitias for a charge? Why were you rewarded for two murders?"

Balthier took a shaky breath. "Maybe because I needed something to cling to, a light to show me a way out of the dark tunnel I was in. Maybe the Onesong thought that I had suffered enough and wanted to give me something good in my life for once. I don't know why I was chosen to train Moonhunter. I certainly have never felt like I deserved him."

"Why did you come with Moonhunter, especially after Mauktil tried to warn you off?"

"Because he is my charge, as you said."

"Nothing more?"

Balthier reached for the Humline once more, hoping to glean what Ralph expected him to say. He'd already apologized, and no words or actions could bring back the dead. After a length, Balthier shook his head. "Nothing more." When he steadied himself, he dragged his gaze up to meet Ralph's eyes. "Was there something you needed from me? A dragon-skinned punching bag maybe?"

Disgust flashed across Ralph's face. It might as well have been an old, flickering neon sign hanging in the window of a dingy bar. "No, what would make you think that? Oh, your file…" He raised the manila folder in his hand, glancing sordidly at it.

Balthier felt his face go placid as he continued to stare at the Wellsdeep Keeper.

Ralph cleared his throat. "I have no need for violence against you, nor do any of the Keepers have ill-will against you."

"Then what is it you want?"

"We need you to commit something no other novihomidrak would dare."

"No." It wasn't even a choice. The tang zipping back along the Humline smacked of deadly betrayal.

"It's only a Shil'mak, and from what I've heard, you don't like them very much."

"I downright hate Shil'maks, but I would never kill one. It's still a dragon and I'm honor bound to them."

"Really?" Ralph leaned back in his chair. "That's not what I've heard. You killed Vehlka in order to save her pevitias. The saperes tried to stop you. Now I point you at one, and a Shil'mak who is crazy and deserves to be put down, and you claim you would never kill a dragon. I would say that you are already experienced at it."

"Experienced? Is that what you call it?"

"Would you rather I call it murder?"

Balthier shook his head. "It doesn't matter what you call it. I won't do it."

"Did you ever ask why a sapere would request this of you?"

"Because you are crazy. Does it run in the family?"

"My cousin died, and there's an insane dragon trying desperately to get into Wellsdeep."

"Is killing the dragon going to bring your cousin back?"

The verbal chess had reached a point where Ralph realized he was not going to get an easy win and that reflected on his face. "No, but the monster that killed my cousin must be destroyed and the Shil'mak dragon must be downed in order to save this world. Do not let my family's sacrifice go in vain."

"Your family's sacrifice?" Balthier repeated slowly. "Why was your uncle pulling a monster out of chaos?" Considering that the Grekish had grabbed Ralph's cousin and murdered her, along with the fact that Dr. Melstone worked with dark matter, the energy where the chaos of the Onesong lived, had the Grekish been called forth for another purpose?

When next Ralph spoke, his calmly soft voice held none of the previous harshness. "At first, I rued the fact that you came with Moonhunter. Then I saw the greater purpose. With your help, with your... actions... as a novihomidrak, we could save this world. Right now, Moonhunter is going after the Grekish. You must go after Rel."

Balthier thought of Moonhunter's desire to help the world. He'd called the boy soft hearted. If Moonhunter was here, offered this same proposal, he knew Moon would take it. Balthier was supposed to be the wiser one, the mentor, but he was not worthy of making a decision like this. Even if training Moonhunter had cleansed his karma, he still had too many disrespectable wounds on his soul. Would saving a planet even balance his deeds?

He and Moonhunter needed to return. He'd take another failure, even if it meant that they institutionalized him. He probably deserved to be locked away. Moonhunter would be elevated to a full novihomidrak. It had been a long time since he needed to be an apprentice; Balthier just didn't want to lose Moonhunter.

"Saving a world, Balthier. Think of it. That's what a novihomidrak lives for."

"How is killing a Shil'mak going to save a world? How will it not bring the Dragon Council down upon my head?"

Ralph stood up, walked to the window, and tugged to release the rolling drapery covering it. As the shade curled around the bar above, the sight of the colliding galaxy came into view. "I won't deny that the Dragon Council won't have some initial irritation, at least outwardly over the death of a dragon, but it'll just be for show, especially with the lives of so many having been saved."

"But how exactly is it going to save those lives?" Balthier insisted.

"With the help of an imagine dragon, we open a new branch of the Well and we tuck this planet inside of it. It'll seem like the ribbon of the approaching galaxy just vanished."

"And no one will find that odd? The people of this planet have seen their imminent doom coming since they were crawling out of caves. They won't just believe it disappears. Certainly the Wellsdeep Keepers know the importance of not letting the masses learn about the dragons, novihomidraks, and saperes. How will you explain it away? Do you plan on altering reality?"

"What happens after we save the world doesn't matter.

Oh, for a few days it'll be mass confusion and hysteria. There will be news filled with conspiracy theories and fear-mongering, but then, all will settle back down and people will begin to forget. They will start to question if there was even a colliding galaxy at all. Within a few generations, the galaxy will be mere footnote. And after that, it will disappear from the books. No one will care. It'll just be all gone. Long term, Balthier. You've seen it yourself. In your long life, did anyone care about what happened to you, or did it get shoved aside and forgotten? You remember, just as this solar system will. But like when the bad people got removed from your life, the inertia that has been started will continue to let the galaxy drift on its path, much as you had the strength to continue on. You rose above your earlier beginnings and became the novihomidrak you were meant to be."

"No. You can't convince me this is for the best."

"Really? A whole planet of people, a thriving and peaceful civilization. Are you going to tell me that's not worth the life of one dragon, a Shil'mak at that."

"I said no."

Ralph sank down in his chair a little as he put his hands behind his head. "Whew! I have to say I'm impressed. I wouldn't have taken you for one who would sacrifice an entire planet for one black dragon. You've got fortitude."

"No. I just keep my thoughts simple. The way I see it, all you need to do is bring an imagination dragon in through the Wells and then carry out your plan. There's no need for the Shil'mak to die."

"I tried." Ralph smacked his hands against the table as he stood up. "I really tried." He walked out the door, leaving Balthier in silence and questions about what all that was about.

The Humline shivered.

20

Moonhunter woke inside a capsule that looked an awful lot like an Airster with the front seats torn out. His hands had been duct taped together before him and his ankles similarly bound. It hadn't been meant to hold him for long, just delay him, but it had enough strength to it that he couldn't rip it apart.

With a shudder, he realized that he was moving; the craft was in the air. He fought to keep his wings from surfacing in a desperate attempt at a flight which he controlled. That was pointless inside a small craft.

Letting his face morph, he used his dragon teeth to slice the binding from around his wrists. The adhesive pulled away from his skin with enough sting to leave a red mark. He next reached down and used his talons to tear away the tape around his legs.

As he scrambled up, an oxygen tank rolled against him. He settled it with a hand on the cool metal. The hose attached to the flow nozzle dragged something with it: a respirator. Yes, the air in here already felt a little thin.

The interior of the defiled Airster darkened and

Moonhunter turned his attention to the front window. He was far enough back that he could still see the stars of distant space at the very top of the growing surface of an object rushing toward him. No, he was speeding toward it. And fast.

He grabbed the controls. It did absolutely nothing.

A feminine voice rang out through the cabin, "Manual controls not yet enabled. Please wait."

Autopilot, again! Somehow, he didn't think that normal Airsters were meant for space flight, even a short trip to the planet's moon. He could hear Balthier laughing at him and the fine mess he'd found himself in this time.

How had they managed to shield their plan from the Humline? Why hadn't he had an inkling?

"Not the time, Moon," he said to himself as the shadowy ridges of the gray moon began to take the shape of mountains. "Oh, damn." Between the sharp peaks and the cratered surface, this was not going to be a smooth landing. He doubted that there were any novihomidrak weapons embedded in the ship that would kill him upon landing, but the question was how long he'd be injured before recovering enough to get figure out why he'd been sent here.

No spacesuit had been provided, which meant the saperes knew there was enough atmospheric pressure for him to survive on the moon's surface as long as he had oxygen to breathe. It also meant enough gravity to hold the atmosphere. But even with all that, time would be preciously short.

Knowing he didn't have a moment to spare, Moon-hunter slipped the strap of the respirator behind his head and settled the mask over his face. He twisted the knob to let a flow of air reach him. The tank had a single strap on it, barely adequate for carrying, but he slung it across his back anyway and let it settle in at a comfortable angle.

The pleasant female voice returned. "Manual controls will engage in ten seconds. Nine… eight… seven…"

Moonhunter glanced around to see if there was any way that he could strap himself, but the craft hadn't been designed for his protection, only his transport.

"Six…" he said in unison with the overhead voice.

Legs bent at the knees, he stood straight enough to stare out the front window. Certainly in preparing the Airster for space travel, a concept he was still having a hard time getting his head around, they had replaced the glass with something a little sturdier. He felt as if he should know what it was called since he'd flown on so many space-ships, but he really had no idea. It had always been a window. If he got through this, he wouldn't be so negligent about the names of things in the future.

"Three… two… one…"

At the accompanying beep, Moonhunter pulled the w-shaped wheel back as hard as he could. The nose of the craft rose. He tried to turn the wheel, a part of him wondering if he could somehow get the Airster to point back and return to the planet. Nothing about this moon, as well as the fact that he only had one tank of air and no food, invited him to stay. For whatever reason he was here, he knew it couldn't be good. In fact, someone blindly shooting him at the moon in a craft like this spoke to the reality that he wasn't expected to return. His task was expected to be a one-way trip.

Yeah, that bothered him.

The ship yawed faintly, but the speed pushed the tail around much faster than expected. A sharp ridgeline of peaks appeared like razors ready to slice the ship open. Moonhunter tried to pull the craft up again.

It seemed hell-bent on crashing into the triangular spires.

He tried to turn.

In no way was he going to make it. He leaned forward and clutched the wheel. He tucked his head down.

The wrenching sound of metal curling around rock tore through the bottom of the craft. The back end rose, sending the ship flipping through the air. It struck another ridge and began spinning.

It took a moment for Moonhunter to realize that every-thing had come to a stopped quiet. When he dared to open his eyes, he still clung to the wheel, though it had broken off the shaft and he now stared up at the top of the craft. Since he lay painfully bent over the tank, the Airster had landed upright, a situation he was thankful for since rolling it over to open the top hatch would have been a difficult task. As it was, his back cracked as he straightened up. A few ribs felt cracked, maybe a broken vertebrae, but nothing serious enough that it wouldn't heal on its own. Still a rueful irritation that made it hard to breathe.

The bones hadn't quite all popped back into place as he reached for the handle labeled *Lift to Release*. A grimace spread across his face as agony fought to draw up the flat bar.

Yes, he now had an idea why Balthier hated saperes.

Checking the security of the respirator's mask, Moon-hunter stepped out of the craft. Looking up, he saw the planet with the brilliant colors of destruction behind it. The colliding galaxy had already torn apart other planets in the solar system and the awesome span of it took Moon-hunter's breath away for a moment, relieving him of the pain in his back for an instant.

He turned to look at the Airster, wondering if it would be in any condition to make a return trip if he could figure out how to do that. It sat in a crevasse, half buried and looking bruised. The hull had been breached, a situation which would make entry into the planet's atmosphere difficult if not impossible, but maybe it would make it just long enough for him to evacuate and use his wings. The metal of the ship already had a shine to it from the heat. He was fairly certain that the Airster was not meant for space travel.

"I thought they rented these things to anyone," he spoke into the respirator.

He felt the cold atmosphere already seeping under his clothes and snuggling close to his skin. Freezing, not something he wanted to experience either.

Why had they sent him here? If the Wellsdeep Keepers wanted him dead, they could have done it while he was unconscious. The Airster had been modified, speaking to the fact they wanted him to reach the moon alive. But why?

A roar drew his attention. He swung around, calling his bow to hand. He held it with a notched arrow already drawn back, thumb against his cheek. There was enough gravity to keep him solidly on the ground, but he'd hadn't walked around enough to get a feel for how much gravity there was or wasn't. He had no idea if he had to fire an arrow, if it would fly straight, soar off, on crash downwards. Too many unknowns.

Whatever had caused the sound wasn't near him.

Yet.

Moonhunter lowered his bow and slipped the arrow into the quiver on his back. He better get comfortable in his surroundings. As soon as he knew all the conditions he was dealing with, the better off he'd be when the source of the noise discovered it was no longer alone on the moon.

He stepped forward, surprised that the atmosphere was

so thick. Did it have anything to do with the colliding galaxy or was the core of the moon denser than he would have imagined? Either way, walking would be slow going.

"Vochey," he spoke heavily into the mask while holding out his hand. His dagger appeared. He stored the weapon away on his belt before returning his hand to the notched arrow.

The ground crunched beneath his footsteps as clods of dirt broke. The crashing of so many meteors into the moon had broken up the land and the atmosphere had held onto the chunky layers beneath a thin top soil.

He blinked down his dragon lids and took another sweeping glance around. What could be living on this dead rock?

Chaos.

The answer rang through to him with ultra-clarity. Chaos could thrive here. Alone, no food, little air… deprivation enhanced chaos.

Crouching low, he moved forward in the direction he recalled the sound coming from. With the abnormal atmosphere, sound wouldn't travel as expected. The roar would probably dissipate faster, meaning the beast that made it would be nearer than he thought.

Had it been the saperes' intent to land him so close?

How much air was in the tank?

He certainly didn't like where his line of questioning was taking him. They didn't want him getting off the moon; that much was very clear to him already. They'd gotten him here and given him just enough air to get the mission done. A return trip was not planned. Neither was a rescue mission, he was sure. But, they also should have realized that if the cold destitution of the moon wasn't enough to kill off the Grekish, then how successful would it be in killing off a novihomidrak?

Could he reason with the Grekish, make friends with it even? He laughed a little at his wonderings, imagining the saperes' faces as he and the Grekisk came back for a little teamed-up revenge.

If only it were ever that easy.

A tingle ran down his back. He was being stalked.

He spun, dropping down on one knee, and raising his drawn bow up in the air.

A beast as black as the space behind it dropped down on him. He fired the arrow. His hand reached for another. Weight impacted with him. They rolled.

Chaos opened its mouth to devour Moonhunter.

21

Listening to the hum of the air circulating through the purifier and fans, Balthier had nearly fallen asleep in his metal chair. When he tried to move his hands to get comfortable enough for slumber, the chains holding him rattled and his skin passed over the cold metal of the table. He couldn't even adjust the cold, metal chair bolted to the floor. All he wanted was respite from this position of holding his hands out before him and the scent of artificially cooled air that stank of a freezer-burned ice cubes.

If he'd just agreed to kill the dragon, at least he'd be free. It didn't mean he actually had to hunt down the Shil'-mak. He could have pretended to be going after it while looking for Moonhunter.

He hated his slow mind. What he wouldn't give to be as quick-witted as Moonhunter. Sitting here, alone, waiting in what felt like suspended time, Balthier regretted every decision which had lead him here. Moonhunter had been right, as always; they should have escaped together.

Footsteps sounded in the hallway outside the door. The handle turned and the door swung open.

Balthier had to guess that the next man coming into the room was a low ranking military officer from the lack of badges or brass on his uniform. He wasn't quite sure what to expect, making him doubly surprised when the man took some keys from his pocket and began unlocking the cuffs holding Balthier to the table. "Let's go," he said in a voice not nearly as gruff as Balthier was expecting. This man seemed full of surprises.

"Where are we going?" Balthier asked back.

"Off base. My instructions are to release you as soon as we are outside the force field. After that, what you do is your own business, but we highly suggest you get yourself off world and back to your own."

"That right? Why?"

"Kill orders, I suspect. You're marked as an enemy of the state now. Not safe for you to be here. Why stay where you're not wanted if you have the option to leave?"

Balthier stood and followed the officer. With his hands still cuffed, they weren't treating him as if he were much of a threat. Might as well let that play out. He looked around as much as he could, taking in the details of the base he saw, without looking like he was actually scoping the place out. He sauntered as much as he could, trying to delay, trying to sense Moonhunter's presence.

As they were nearly out of the building, Balthier saw Ralph talking to a sapere. "Hey, where's Moonhunter?" he shouted.

Ralph glanced casually over his shoulder at Balthier, then returned to his conversation with the sapere.

Balthier moved in their direction, making the officer he was with change course suddenly. "Where's Moon?"

The officer grabbed his arm and tugged him back.

Balthier wasn't going to let this go. He fought against the officer's hold.

"Where's Moonhunter?" Balthier hollered again.

Ralph broke away and walked toward Balthier. He motioned with his hand for the officer to release the novi-homidrak and back up a bit. "Moonhunter is gone. He has been sent away from here. Go home."

"Where's he gone? Where did you send him?"

"Nowhere that you will be able to help him. He is on his own."

That familiar tingle from the Humline ran through Balthier again. "Where is he?"

"He's on the moon. He has truly become a hunter on the moon. He's going after the Grekish."

"You sent him after the Grekish? Alone?"

Ralph shrugged. "You had your chance to help. You denied it. Officer Madison, take him out of here. Deadly force is authorized." He started back toward the sapere once more.

The officer tugged Balthier along.

"Get me there," Balthier yelled as he tugged away from the officer. "Let me go help Moon."

"There is no help for Moonhunter. It was a one-way trip. His trip took all the resources we had. We don't have enough to get you there as well, or for Moonhunter to return."

Balthier morphed, his dragon teeth coming down, claws extending. His dragon lids cast a red color over the room, sharpening details. "There has to be a way. Let me help Moonhunter take on this Grekish. He's an apprentice and can't do it alone."

Ralph jerked his head. "The mission is done. And so is yours."

Balthier felt a sharp jab in his side, along with a jolt of

electricity. He began to turn, ready to mock the wielder. The shock dragon tail was weakening. It would take more than that to bring down a creature like him... wait, what was he called? Balthier's world spun out from beneath him as he began to fall.

Feeling displaced from his own body as he started to slip to the floor, Balthier realized too late that the shock dragon had only been the means of delivery for a tranquilizer. The shock wasn't supposed to be extremely potent, but rather a distracting way to puncture the hide of a novihomidrak. He hit the floor, bounced, then skipped away into the blackness waiting to welcome him.

When he woke, the startle brought him to a sitting position. His novihomidrak aspects responded to the alarm. He growled, bringing himself to his hands and knees, one hand raised to attack with his extended claws. A flood of memories from long ago conflicted with his thoughts about where he was now.

The nearby birds and crickets grew quiet.

The dark silence calmed him enough to gain awareness of where he was. They no longer had him at the compound. He was outside. On grass. Among many trees as far as he could see in every direction even with his dragon vision.

A sight through the branches caught his attention.

The moon glowed a pale white in the nighttime sky above.

Moonhunter was there. And Balthier was here, now outside the military compound. He couldn't help Moonhunter from here.

But there might be someone who could. Unfortunately, it was a Shil'mak.

Balthier got to his feet. Time to go talk to this crazy dragon.

22

oonhunter loosened the arrow into the beast as
it tried to glom onto him. The tip went solidly
into its chest. The beast didn't scream in pain,
as Moonhunter wished, but it did take a step backwards.
But whether that was because of the force of the arrow's
flight or because of the injury itself, Moonhunter wasn't
certain.

Either way, it gave him an opportunity to break free
from their tumble. He jumped to his feet, backed up
another couple steps, and drew another arrow. Then a
third, and fourth. Soon, he had a good half dozen arrows
into the monster.

But it didn't fall. Rather, it looked more than just a little
unhappy.

It charged for Moonhunter.

He slung the bow over his shoulder. He reached for the
dagger in the belt at his side. His fingers closed around the
freezing metal of the hilt. The cold stung, but he had to
hold onto the weapon.

Bringing up his hands, Moonhunter lodged the dagger

into the monster. At first, the weapon resisted as if the beast had some sort of armor, natural or otherwise, around it. Then the blade sank deep.

"Fas'co chilstrada raktu." The dagger began to glow deep red and grew so hot that Moonhunter wondered if he'd have to release the handle.

The monster still made no noise, though it did struggle as if trying to get off the blade.

It struck Moonhunter, sending him flying backwards. He landed tank first on the ground and skid.

"Vochey, Serenity," he shouted into the respirator. Hand out as if reaching toward the beast, Moonhunter willed his dagger to return. It didn't.

As he tried to roll, he found the tank lying across his bow, holding it down at an angle to make it more like a crossbar so that he couldn't move. He couldn't sit up either.

The Grekish had given up trying to get the dagger out of its abdomen. In exchange, it stormed toward Moonhunter. He watched it come, his breathing getting shallow. If he and Tranquility could survive the onslaught attack without either one of them breaking, and if he found himself in a position to get to his feet, he might have a chance.

The ground trembled beneath the Grekish's feet.

Nope, there was no way Moonhunter would survive. Not with his arrows scattered all over the ground and the beast bending down to pick several of them up. A plan. He needed a plan.

The Grekish grunted as it lifted a fistful of arrows, many jutting out between his fingers in different directions like someone pulling out a handful of toothpicks. It wouldn't even matter if the monster had a clumsy aim;

with arrows at every angle, one was bound to strike Moonhunter.

Rotating his shoulder, he slipped free of the harness holding the tank to his back and rolled. The arm still looped through the other strap dragged the tank with him. He knew he needed it, but it hampered his ability to fight.

The Grekish slammed the arrows down into the gray dirt, spewing grit in all directions. It surreally floated as if given a life of its own that he and the Grekish seemed to watch.

Moonhunter dragged the tank up and across his chest. He rammed it into the side of the beast's head. The atmosphere didn't allow him the force he was used to. He might as well have been trying to strike a wasp with a feather.

Moonhunter rolled over again, this time landing with his chest upon the tank. He pushed himself up. Holding the straps, he flung the tank wide. The reach of it pulled on the hose attached to his mask. For a moment, he thought he might lose his respirator and the cool flow of oxygen.

The Grekish roared with pain and anger. His recovery to charge didn't seem to take nearly long enough. Moonhunter had been hoping for several more minutes so that he could get out of here. Instead, his retreat came in the form of flying backwards through the air after being backhanded.

The strap of the mask broke and the respirator flew off. Moonhunter landed without the tank following him and barrel rolled several feet until coming to a stop on his stomach.

He heard low chuckle and lifted his face off the ground to look. The Grekish approached.

Moonhunter pressed to his feet and once again tried to call his dagger. This time it came.

"Come on now," he said into the thin air. It wasn't quite as bad as he was expecting. The denser gravity also gave this satellite a little bit more of an atmosphere than most moons. "We don't have to do this."

"Chaos," it returned.

He couldn't drag enough air into his chest. Missing the oxygen, he felt his arms and legs beginning to ache.

"Yes, chaos. Why don't we put that idea in a box and shove it out an airlock? Chaos, my friend, just isn't any good." Moonhunter waved the dagger in front of him, hoping the distant sun would glint off his blade and scare the Grekish. The blade didn't intimidate the beast at all.

To Moonhunter's surprised, the Grekish began to laugh. "I have devoured many worlds, little dragon boy. What makes you think this one is different?"

Holding his dagger aloft, Moonhunter reached down for the mask. He took a deep breath, surprised that air was still coming through the hose, then said, "Little dragon boy? Well, that's a first for me."

"Go home, little dragon, back to your world. This one is doomed to die, even without my help. I can end their pain before it comes."

Moonhunter worked at tying the two ends of the strap together. "See, I'm just not ready to give up on them yet. I've seen some pretty amazing things happen out there in the universe. I'll keep my faith that this galaxy can be saved too."

"Not going to happen. Chaos wins."

He slipped the strap over his head. "Whatever," he muttered before sliding the mask in place over his mouth and nose.

"Already your body gets cold and your air supply won't

last long," the Grekish taunted. "Things like that don't matter to me."

Moonhunter jerked his thumb in the direction of the downed Airster. "One way trip. I don't think I'm going back. I might as well accept the battle with you." His words were so muffled behind his mask that he barely understood them; he wasn't certain he cared if the Grekish comprehended them or not. He reached down for the tank and slung it over his shoulders.

"Beg for death."

"You first."

The Grekish charged.

Moonhunter drew his bow, drawing back the string with a notched arrow he pulled from the ground. A crisp twang came from the sinew. He retrieved another arrow from the moon's surface and fired. He got off a third shot before falling into the Grekish's lumbering reach.

The Grekish's breath stank like a putrid mass grave as the monster of chaos yanked Moonhunter close. Certain as he was that a normal human wouldn't be able to smell it beneath the respirator, Moonhunter silently cursed the strength of his novihomidrak senses.

Moonhunter buried Serenity into the Grekish's belly.

The Grekish released Moonhunter with a shove. The weapon stayed in Moonhunter's hand, the blade sliding from its victim's flesh. The Grekish staggered backwards, gasping and reeling, clutching at its wound.

Then it started to laugh.

The triumphant feeling vanished from Moonhunter.

Removing its hands from the spot where the injury should have been, the Grekish slapped its thighs, bending over in peals of laughter. "Oh, I've been wounded. I'm stabbed. Dying."

Then the Grekish straightened, seriousness overtaking

its boulder-like features. "No, I'm not. Not that easy, little dragon."

It charged again, head forward, lanky arms reaching.

Moonhunter got two more shots fired from Tranquility before noticing the bow was useless. The arrows stuck in the Grekish's hide for only a moment before falling away. Novihomidrak weapons were no use against it.

Moonhunter turned and ran.

He wondered if there was any way to get the Airster to overcharge and explode. How long would that take to set up? Far too long, he felt certain. Besides, he could feel the planet beginning to block the sun from hitting the moon and the thin atmosphere grew chillier by the moment. As soon as the planet blocked the sun, he suspected it would get very cold. There was absolutely nothing on this barren rock that would let him survive the night.

No way out.

He wished Balthier was here and missing the older man so suddenly brought tears to his eyes. Balthier would know what needed to be done. Balthier would touch the Humline and know how to defeat this enemy. Moonhunter didn't trust his own senses.

He wanted to stop, to give up. There was no way this ended well for him. Why fight the inevitable?

He sensed the Grekish behind him. Moonhunter turned, dropping to his knees while thrusting the dagger upwards. It caught in the Grekish's abdomen. Moonhunter lifted the monster, flipping the chaos beast over him in a rush of instinct and adrenaline.

Moonhunter wanted to stop fighting. Why couldn't he? "Balthier," he whispered as the Grekish hit the ground. He wished the word would bring the man here as if magically by command. He couldn't do this alone.

Anguish ripped from his throat. He couldn't do this alone. "Balthier!"

23

Balthier used the Humline to follow Rel's energy to the dragon's den. Not surprisingly, Rel had blasted a hole in the center of the forest, leaving a large crater now worn by age. Some dragons started lairs with their breath, then dug out chambers with their talons. Some only used their breath to clear away debris. He wondered, as he stood looking at the rounded mound before him, which Rel had done.

Scrambling up the short hillside, Balthier saw the other side had been blasted away into a long, sloping tunnel. There would be no other way but to slide down its length. Hoping to control his descent, he started down. As the tunnel darkened, it got steeper. Balthier blinked down his dragon lids, making it a little easier for him to see the cracks in the crag he climbed.

At the bottom where it leveled out, Balthier saw signs of digging. The scent of freshly turned earth indicated it was recent. Hidden as lumpy masses of shadows, rubble had been pushed to the sides of the tunnel, enough to clear the way for the dragon and giving Balthier a good sized path to walk down. At each twist and turn in the path, Balthier hesitated, pausing to give his full attention to the way ahead with his hearing, sight, and connection to the Humline. Rel could be waiting and ready to fry an intruder.

"Back again, novi?" the dragon grumbled from somewhere further down the darkened tunnels.

So Moonhunter had already spoken to Rel, and now, because both he and Moonhunter shared the same novimather, the dragon confused Balthier's energy for Moonhunter's. Now he only had to hope that Moonhunter hadn't irritated Rel.

"Rocktae shaul, honorable dragon," Balthier called out in greeting.

"You are not the novihomidrak who I spoke to earlier!"

At least Rel could tell their voices apart. That actually leaned toward the dragon being fairly sane. That was a good sign. "I am not, but I was also born from Vehlka of the Ch'bauldi." He hoped that would bear some weight with Rel. Having respect for one's parents generally gained favor among people and dragons both. "I have come in hopes of getting your help."

Though he couldn't feel it along the floor, a ripple in the current moving through the tunnels let Balthier know that Rel was moving toward him. Sneaky. Small and stealthy this dragon was.

"What are my chances of that happening?" Balthier called out when the dragon said nothing. He couldn't think of anything else to say which would force the dragon to speak. Rel wanted to remain silent. Balthier would hear him getting closer and they both knew it.

The ebbing current felt more like a pulse now.

Still no sound from the dragon.

Maybe it was crazy, insane enough to want to destroy a novihomidrak.

Balthier pulled Disharmony from the holster at his side and braced his arms while keeping the barrel pointed at the floor of the tunnels. If the dragon meant harm, at least he'd get a decent shot off first.

"Rel?" Might as well give the dragon one last chance.

Balthier put his back to the wall, sliding sideways as he approached the oncoming corner to a new tunnel.

He felt Rel on the other side.

The dragon breathed raggedly.

Emotional pain flooded through Balthier like nothing he'd felt before. He hated the silence. "Please! This is Moonhunter. He's my apprentice and barely a boy. I need your help."

"Come forward, novi."

The voice came from much further back than Balthier had imagined. But if it hadn't been the dragon, what else could it have been.

Balthier rounded the corner, raising his gun as he went just in case.

The tunnel was empty.

Except for the magic. Rel had stayed further back, reaching out toward him with a spell to reveal why Balthier was really there. Somehow, the dragon had managed to cloak the spell behind the Humline so that it felt more like the dragon moving forward. Very sneaky.

"Put your weapon away, novi. Be calm and know you are safe. Understand my reasons that I had to be sure you intended no treachery."

Balthier holstered Disharmony and pulled his jacket over it. "Because I could very well have been coming here to kill you. The Humline didn't let you know what I had decided." It was a guess, but he figured he might as well lay it all out on the table.

He couldn't believe he was trying to gain the trust of a Shil'mak.

"Your devotion to your apprentice is what makes you a wildcard. I'm not even sure you had fully made your decision when you entered my lair."

Now it was Balthier's turn to remain silent. If he had to admit the truth to himself, no, he hadn't fully decided if he'd take the Wellskeeper's offer or not.

"I figured you to be the boy though," Rel continued. "The possibility that he would side with the saperes was great too."

The dragon's voice was so close now and Balthier knew as soon as he rounded the corner he'd be face-to-snout with the beast. Balthier paused for a moment. There was something more in Rel's words which had gone unspoken: if the dragon mixed up Balthier with Moonhunter, that meant that helping Moonhunter had eased the dark taint of his soul, and even more, Moonhunter hid something from Balthier. The only way to balance out the shadow of Balthier's energy would be the keeping of a deep secret on Moonhunter's part. He thought of his apprentice always going off to his room after they completed a mission. Meditating or some such nonsense, Moonhunter had always led Balthier to believe. What if it was something more? Drugs? Was it possible that Moon was dabbling in the drug market? Running shipments between planets even?

Balthier couldn't even focus enough to reach out with the thought to the Onesong. There were so many ways to make illicit money, so many secrets that Moonhunter could be keeping, and Balthier only wanted his apprentice back safely. Whatever Moonhunter was hiding, Balthier didn't really care as long as the boy was safe. Everything else could be dealt with.

He hated this planet. Nothing good ever happened here.

Balthier rounded the corner.

Rel lounged against the far wall, his legs tucked beneath him and his wings relaxed. "What trouble has the boy apprentice found?"

Balthier tried to bow at the waist, but he only went a quarter of the way. How was he to trust a Shil'mak to help him? Surely Rel would see the disrespect running completely through Balthier. "The Wellskeepers have sent Moonhunter to fight the Grekish."

"Then he has been sent to his death. You know there can be no coming back from that."

"I realize this planet has no trustworthy interplanetary travel. How would they get him there? They must believe there is atmosphere of some kind on the moon. What would they have sent him with?"

Rel's head lowered a bit. "Their Airsters have very strong engines. Chances are they have modified those. The Wellskeepers do have the knowledge of the novihomidraks coming to this planet through the ages, as well as their various assignments, so it's not like they have no knowledge of space and the hazards. But the moon is untested, so the environment undetermined. They know the Grekish lives there and there must be some atmosphere. Chances are that the Wellskeepers are making a vast guess."

"How does the Grekish move from the moon to the planet?"

Rel's mouth split into a toothy grin. "Did they tell you the truth?"

"About?"

"About the scientist's daughter?"

Balthier stepped forward. He lowered his head in shame. "The Wellskeeper I spoke to, Ralph, said it was his cousin who was grabbed by the Grekish. It was my fault that she was down there."

Rel's head drew back as he hissed. "Do not let them shame you. They did not tell you everything."

"What have they left out?"

"Not only was the cousin a Wellskeeper, but she was a ninja too."

Balthier felt as if the floor of the cave shuddered beneath him. "How is that even possible?"

"I was betrayed."

"You were the one who blessed her as a sapere?"

"I blessed the whole family. They wanted more. They knew how much prestige there was in being saperes, let alone Wellskeepers."

"Saperes are generally not from the same family," Balthier confirmed.

"That wasn't enough." Rel shook his head. "They found a ninja to train her."

"Wouldn't that have negated her protection against chaos?"

"It did more than that; it called the chaos to come take her. The Grekish came to pull her forever into the shadows, and devour her it did."

"But Dr. Melstone and his nephew, Ralph, both think that the way to save her is to kill you. Why?"

Rel shifted on the floor. "There is a reason that those who train to be ninjas are removed from their families, why they are turned into outcasts."

"Not all ninjas are soulcolists first," Balthier corrected, knowing that most ninjas started out in training to collect the souls of the dead. Being taught how to work with death energy naturally turned those students into an aberration most other people didn't want to be around.

"But most are orphans. Very few have familial connections," Real said.

"You think that the chaos fed back through her to them? That their minds have been warped and bent to the Grekish's will?"

"I have no solid proof, but that is a theory."

"So you would destroy the entire family?"

Rel tilted his large head. "You believe any of them are innocent?"

"I would say that if you are going to presume guilt over all of them, you should take your own share."

Once again, Rel's head lifted sharply, nearly slamming into ceiling of the cave. "My guilt?"

Balthier pointed his finger toward Rel, hoping to drive home his point with the dragon. "With your connection to the Onesong, you had to ignore some sign. You can't tell me that you received no indication of their betrayal. I don't believe it."

"You would make me all-knowing?"

"I think the dragons sometimes ignore the signs they receive, unable to believe that someone might not be as noble as they are. But not everyone has your high standards." Balthier charged forward several steps, his index finger still pointing accusingly. "What you ignore makes you susceptible to the chaos. It leaves many people hurting and I think you remain in denial about your part in the injuries inflicted upon others."

Rel nodded slowly. "Does your connection to the Onesong make you invincible to errors? Have you not learned in your many years that sometimes the actions of other go differently than predicted? Why would you, our offspring, assume that our connection would be any stronger than yours?"

"Because you're supposed to be better than us. You tell us where to go, who to save, and we do it. But who comes to save us?" Balthier felt tears starting to roll from his eyes, across his cheeks, and into his graying beard. "Who helps us?"

The dragon closed his eyes and remained quiet for a long moment. Balthier ran his hands across his face, scrubbing his skin dry of the tears. Of all the dragons that he would break down in front of, why did it have to be a Shil'mak? He turned himself away, ready to walk from the cave the moment he thought he could do so without a tremor in his step.

"Revenge was not enough, was it?" Rel asked right as Balthier found the strength to leave.

"No."

"Has it helped to finally be able to yell at a dragon? Do you feel vindicated?"

"No." In truth, Balthier felt smaller than ever, puny and unjustified standing before the Shil'mak. "No."

"Do you not think I feel exactly the same way when I think of how Dr. Melstone betrayed me? I do not dare catch Melstone when I chase him because I know that revenge is not the answer. Yes, I do hope to scare him, goad him into making a mistake, one that will be his own undoing, but I do not believe the Onesong would let me be a very good judge for his deeds. I must trust the Onesong to enact the punishment it feels fits the betrayal."

"Don't tell me you think that I should leave Moon-hunter to the Onesong's judgement."

"Is that what you fear, novihomidrak? That I believe all outcomes should be left to the Onesong?"

Balthier shifted, wishing he could roll off his itching

skin. "I don't say what dragons believe. That's not my place."

Rel chuckled. "Gained some wisdom in your years, have you? Come on, out with it."

"No." Balthier pointed his index finger at the dragon again. "You come out with it. Are you going to help me or not?"

24

Light seeped fast away from the surface of the moon. Only a peek of the sun's rays glistened yellow around the edge of the planet. Moonhunter shivered in the growing cold. Would he freeze tonight to wake tomorrow? Did he have the strength to end his own life on Serenity before that happened?

Lukewarm wetness soaked into his pants. He could smell blood.

With the Grekish wounded beside him, Moonhunter awoke to the realization that the beast's blood flowed over the cold rock and now pooled around him. There was still battle to be had here. He couldn't decide what to do with his own life until he'd ended the Grekish's.

Gritting his teeth, Moonhunter pulled the dagger from the Grekish's hide, then stabbed it again. He flung his arm over, half rolling over, in order to accomplish the task.

The Grekish roared and tried to lash out at Moonhunter's arm.

He scrambled, once more dragging the dagger from the Grekish.

The beast tried to move. Moonhunter rolled, pushing up on his hands and toes. His feet scrapped over the grit of the moon, digging into the loose, thick sand that covered it. Only one palm pressed against the ground as the other clutched the dagger's hilt. He crawled forward in his awkward position and fell on top of the Grekish, trying to gain an advantage.

The Grekish seized Moonhunter and shoved the novi-homidrak into the air. Moonhunter swung the dagger, trying to slice anything before he was thrust away. The toss sent Moonhunter rolling. The dagger fell from Moonhunter's hand.

With a growl, the Grekish pounced on Moonhunter, who lay face down. With their positions now reversed, the Grekish grabbed Moonhunter's hair and yanked his head back. Moonhunter pulled his arms in and beneath him, trying to push upward to relieve the growing pressure on his back. The Grekish's weight tipped, the beast becoming unbalanced.

Realizing his opponent reached for the dagger, Moonhunter shoved as hard as he could. The Grekish's arm came around him. Though he tried to resist, Moonhunter found himself lugged with his back against the Grekish's chest. While once more on top of his enemy, he felt more exposed than ever. Especially in the next moment where he saw the glint of his dagger raised above him moments before the Grekish thrust it into Moonhunter's belly.

Moonhunter crunched over, his body coming around the impaling metal. The Grekish responded by holding him tighter. His legs suddenly restless with the pain bolting down them, Moonhunter kicked out.

"Die, little dragon," the Grekish purred in his ear as it pulled the respirator mask away from Moonhunter's face.

Moonhunter rocked in a manic attempt to untangle himself from his enemy. His slick fingers glided half-heartedly over the metal hilt and the Grekish's arm. Everything felt cold and wet. His chest barely breathed of the thin atmosphere.

He would die here. It was going to happen.

The thought brought an anger-forged fighting spirit back to him. He would not go down without taking the Grekish with him. There was still battle to be had here.

"Vochey, Tranquility," he called out. He discarded the bow that came to his hand, reaching instead for the arrows. Taking one up, he speared the Grekish's leg just beneath his own thighs.

The Grekish bucked beneath Moonhunter. The arrows rolled from his grasping fingers as he tried to pick up another. Finally he managed to claw another into his palm. He passed it to the other hand while the Grekish squeezed tighter on his ribcage. He jammed it into his enemy's other leg, inflicting enough pain that the hold loosened enough for him to draw in another breath.

As he reached for a third arrow, he found the Grekish's arm in the way.

"Like arrows?" The Grekish lifted a whole handful above Moonhunter. It felt like de-ja-vu, except that this time the Grekish held him trapped face up to look at the descending arrows and, beyond that, the stars held within the blackness of space. There would be no dodging the arrows now.

His chest ached terribly from the venomcur spilling into his system. He wouldn't make it to a sapere in time. No way he was getting off this rock. Death might just be easier. At least he'd get to watch the stars as he faded from the Onesong.

But only if he took the Grekish down with him.

Moonhunter caught the Grekish's arm as the arrow-filled hand came down on him. He felt the sharp, pointed tips against his chest. Fighting to raise the hand away from him, Moonhunter growled low and deep. It still felt weak and not nearly backed with enough air.

The Grekish released Moonhunter so that it could put both hands around the arrows. Now Moonhunter could push up against the Grekish with all his might while digging his feet into the Grekish's legs. Hoisting up his hips, Moonhunter slid down the Grekish and released the beast-'sarms. The arrows came straight down into the Grekish's chest, barely missing Moonhunter's head.

While the Grekish screamed in rage, Moonhunter rolled away and scooted as far away from his enemy as he could. He pulled the dagger from his chest, the pain-filled screams coming from his own throat now. He flailed, half flopping like a landed fish. He knew he needed to get away from the Grekish, but movement brought agony tearing through him, which made his muscles tremble, which brought more pain and reminded him of his need to get away. The cycles felt endless, though he knew it probably was an extremely short period of time. He seemed only feet away from the Grekish when he heard the monster of chaos issue one final gasp and its eyes went flat.

Moonhunter stared at it, certain that it couldn't be dead. No, his enemy was faking. Chaos always lied.

At length, he reached out and prodded the Grekish with a finger. The beast didn't move. He rolled partially back over, blood dripping from the wound like an abundant stream. He pushed harder on the Grekish. Still, no movement. He slammed down his fist on it, yet there was no response, only a wiggle coming from the multitude of arrows standing from its chest.

Moonhunter flopped back and stared at the sky. Overhead, the planet seemed to be rising, casting shining white light like a halo around it.

No one would know he'd met his end here.

"Balthier," he whispered, feeling a trickle of blood running from his mouth. "I'm here."

25

"I'm here," Balthier's deep voice came, cutting through the darkness surrounding Moonhunter.

The scent of blooming florals and wide fresh air filled his senses. Feeling a thick hand around his, Moonhunter tried to drag open his eyes. The white ceiling came into focus first, then Balthier's face moved into view.

Balthier smiled, a wry, craggily cut through his graying beard.

"Where am I?" Moonhunter attempted to ask, but his voice cracked and gave out. His throat felt terribly raw and forcing the breath out hurt his chest. He quickly decided not to do it again.

"We're back at the shrine. You're safe. The saperes were working on you. Serchk and Sundancer were here too. They've gone now to let you rest."

Moonhunter tried to nod his understanding, but his eyes slipped closed and he fell back into the odd tumble of dreams he'd been having.

He knew it was later when he woke again, though how exactly he knew that more time had passed, he wasn't certain. Balthier slept in a chair beside his bed. Good, Balthier needed his sleep. Moonhunter drifted off for a second interval of rest.

The birds singing outside woke him the third time. His eyes popped open and he felt himself on high alert. He sat up. "The Grekish?" This time the words weren't quite as painful.

Balthier rushed and put his hands on Moonhunter's shoulders to keep him from rising.

Moonhunter glanced around the room. Red curtains fluttered lightly in the window opened to let the breeze in. The antiseptic scent of medical supplies wafted from where they sat on a stand nearby. It wasn't one of the med rooms, but a private quarters transformed for a healing patient to get rest while mending.

He sensed others in the room and expected to see the monster of chaos. Serchk and Sundancer knelt on the pillows on the floor, both stopping in their offering of prayer for Moonhunter's recovery to stare back at him now.

"The Grekish? Where is it?" Moonhunter asked.

"Dead. It's dead."

Moonhunter raised the thin shirt someone had put on him to wear while he was recovering and found a scar where the dagger had entered his chest. "Why am I not dead?" He glanced up to find Balthier's sad eyes locked on his face. "What happened?"

Balthier's eyes teared up. Blinking, he straightened and turned away. With a motion toward Serchk and Sundancer, Balthier urged them both to leave now.

Moonhunter waited for the door to close after his friends left. As much as he wanted to see and visit with them, he needed answers first. "Balthier? Why am I not dead?"

Balthier took a couple strides away and placed his hand against the wall above a bureau with a stainless steel top.

"Tell me what happened?"

Balthier turned back, as if Moonhunter's latest question was easier to answer than the former. "I spoke to Rel. I convinced him that he needed to help you. He teleported us to the moon, but you had already dispatched the beast. We took you back to the planet. The venomcur…"

"What, Balthier? What? It didn't kill me because I'm here now."

"You were very close to succumbing. Rel opened the Wells and brought us home. Not bad for a Shil'mak."

"So Rel's here?" Moonhunter wanted to see him. He threw back the blankets to uncover his legs and started to swing them off the bed. Balthier rushed back to stop him. He covered Moonhunter back up.

"You didn't survive the trip back through the Wells," Balthier confessed.

"What?" He gasped the word, nearly choking on it.

Balthier shook his head. "You were dead."

Fear made a tight swirl in his stomach that tingled all the way to his fingers and toes. "How was I resuscitated?"

Balthier sat down on the corner of the bed, leaning forward over one arm as he gave Moonhunter a level look. "Rel gave up the last of his magic for you. He sacrificed himself so that you would live."

Moonhunter felt tears on his cheeks. "Why? I'm not as important as a dragon. The Wells need the dragons, not me."

"Apparently Rel thought otherwise. Old and crazy dragon."

"Damn dragons," Moonhunter said.

Balthier snickered. "Damn dragons." He leaned over and hugged Moonhunter. It took him a moment after he backed off before he could speak again. "The saperes feel it is time to elevate you, that you no longer need to be my apprentice."

"I'm not ready," Moonhunter admitted.

"You are, whether you feel ready or not."

Recalling how he had called out desperately for Balthier while he'd been on the moon, he reached over and took his mentor's hand. His novimather had placed him with Balthier. "Do you really feel this way, or are you saying that because the saperes want it to be time?"

Balthier's brown eyes returned to Moonhunter. "I still need you," Balthier confessed as he squeezed Moonhunter's fingers. "But you must do what is right for you."

"I still need you as well."

"Then you will remain my apprentice for a while longer, regardless of what the saperes think." Balthier rose, went to the bureau where he opened the top drawer, and gathered clothes for Moonhunter. "Get dressed. We will go."

Glancing to the door his friends had exited only moments ago, Moonhunter wished for a visit with Serchk and Sundancer. He'd come very close to never seeing them again. "Balthier, there's something I should tell you."

"It can wait until we're out flying in space. I think it's time for a little vacation, don't you agree? We'll take a break from saving the universe, have a little relaxation, let you get good and healed. We can talk then."

"No, it's something I should tell you now, something I've been keeping from you for a long time."

Balthier's arms dropped. Pale and clutching an armload of clothes, he sagged back toward the chair and sat down. "Yeah, kid, we probably both have things to say. Things that the other really needs to know."

"And I need to say my thoughts now. Two dragons have given their lives for me. That has to mean something."

"It does. You are very special, not only a pevitias of the dragons, but special to people you save."

Balthier looked as if he wanted to say more, but Moonhunter interrupted. "I want to be the best novihomidrak I can be. It's the only way I can make sure to help everyone who needs it. I want to perform the Crossing."

If it were possible for Balthier to go even more white, he did so now. "That's what you've been hiding from me."

Moonhunter nodded. His ashamed gaze slid off to a corner of the room. "Serchk and Sundancer have been helping me with it."

"Moon, I know they are your friends, but they've only just become saperes. You need saperes who understand what they are doing for the Crossing."

"I know."

"And there are many who would want to abuse their power in the ceremonies so that they could control you."

"Which is why I want my friends to help," Moonhunter said, "and I want you to guard me. I cannot do this without you. I've seen why you don't trust saperes and I've come to understand those feelings. I'd like you to watch out for me while I go through this transformation."

Balthier sat with his thoughts for a moment before he slowly started to nod. "I've come to understand that there are people out there who want to help us. We may not see what they are doing or even know of their efforts. But it's harder if we think we are struggling alone. You're not alone, Moonhunter. If you want to perform the Crossing and become a better novihomidrak, then I am here for you. That is exactly where Vehlka wanted me to be."

"Thank you," Moonhunter said, knowing the words

were such a minimal way to express his relief. "What was it that you wanted to tell me?"

Balthier shook his head now. "It's not important, certainly not compared to you wanting to endure the Crossing. I've made myself into a better novihomidrak and that's what matters. Now, are you ready for our next adventure?" Balthier pitched the clothes he'd gathered toward Moonhunter.

Moonhunter caught his clothes. "Yes."

"Then get dressed. We'll get your sapere friends and go off world for a bit," Balthier said as rose from the chair and headed for the door. "The Wells await us."

Find Moonhunter in These Stories

Or Get Three Bundled Stories

WWW.MORNINGSKYSTUDIOS.COM

WANT MORE NOVIHOMIDRAKS?

FIND THESE TITLES AND MORE AT
WWW.MORNINGSKYSTUDIOS.COM

READY FOR ANOTHER QUEST?

Sign up for Dawn Blair's newsletter to learn about new releases, get access to fun and free stuff, hear about events, and more!

It's easy.

Go to **www.dawnblair.com/newsletter** to join the adventure and get a free PDF of the reading order to Dawn's books.

The courage to become legendary.

WHEN HELPING A PRINCESS TO FIND THREE LOST BOOKS,
HE NEVER EXPECTED TO MAKE SUCH ENEMIES.

Discover the magic in the epic fantasy adventure of the
Sacred Knight series

Start the series with Quest for the Three Books

Use **Wellskeeper10%** at www.morningskystudios.com
for 10% off your purchase.

Find now at your favorite bookstore or visit us online at
www.morningskystudios.com

Use **Wellskeeper10%** for 10% off your purchase.

ABOUT THE AUTHOR

Dawn Blair grew up on a ranch in a rural Nevada town. The old buildings provided inspiration for her imagination as she thrived on stories of unicorns, princesses, heroic knights, and hidden doors to other dimensions.

For as long as she can remember, Dawn has had a passion for storytelling. Though she started out writing, her creative life expanded into painting and illustration.

She loves creating worlds and spinning tales for people to enjoy. The best ones are the stories that surprise her as she's writing. She loves her characters doing the unexpected. She'll gladly tell you that the most exciting part about being a writer is being the first one on the journey.

Thank you for taking the time to join her on these adventures.

Find more about Dawn's work at:
www.morningskystudios.com

facebook.com/dawnblairbooks

x.com/dawnblair

instagram.com/dawn.blair

www.ingramcontent.com/pod-product-compliance
Lightning Source LLC
Chambersburg PA
CBHW071328250626
47159CB00004B/1518